A PROMISE TO KEEP

BOOK ONE OF THE CALDWELL SERIES

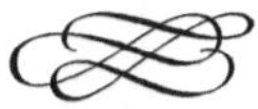

LAUREL WENSON

PROLOGUE

Teagan had always loved the cemetery – until the angel showed up. Now she stood there, glaring at the concrete form perched on top of the gravestone. Her best friend's gravestone.

"She wasn't supposed to die, damn it! Best friends aren't supposed to die in 8th grade!" The angel remained silent, looking down toward her underground charge, hands eternally folded in prayer.

Teagan fell to her knees onto crunchy autumn leaves and stared at her best friend's name – Joanne. "I can't believe you've been gone a year. Why couldn't you have listened to me? To any of us?" She reached out and touched the engraved date with her fingers. "Why did you have to die?"

Her tears felt warm on her cold cheeks. She sobbed as leaves briskly rustled past her. She sniffled as they caught her attention. "Remember how we used to walk through the leaves this time of year? God, this was one of our favorite places. And now I hate it. And I try really hard not to hate you."

She got up and pulled a crumbled piece of paper out of her pocket and opened it, thrusting it out toward the stone. "See this? The damn audition notice came out this week. Our first high school musical together – that's freshman year was supposed to be. That's what we talked about since our first play in fourth grade!"

"And *you!* You laid there in that damn hospital bed last year and made me promise that I'd still try out for shows without you. 'Make a new friend,' you said. 'Everything will be fine,' you said."

She had started pacing back and forth over the grave. "Well, I got news for ya! I'll never get on a stage again, and I'll never have another friend like you – aside from Brian. I wouldn't have made it through this year without him – and therapy."

She crumbled the paper back up and threw it on the ground, watching as it rolled across the lawn like a tumbleweed amidst the leaves. She wiped her tears and stood defiantly in front of the angel. "So you just stay here with your angel friend – maybe she'll hum show tunes with you. 'Cause my theater days died right along with you. Instead of trying out, you know what I did? I went out and got a job. Working with a bunch of old people that I'll never care about – and they'll never hurt me."

"So happy anniversary, bestie." Her words were thick as she turned to leave. "Thanks for the worst year of my life."

CHAPTER 1

As the school bus passed by the cemetery Teagan looked out the window at the lawn blanketed with red and yellow leaves. Toward the back of the cemetery she could see where the angel perched on top of her best friend's gravestone. Her eyes still got misty thinking back to the hardest goodbye.

"Teags, you okay?"

She blinked back the tears and nodded, looking to the concerned face that sat next to her as they rode past the cemetery.

"I miss her, too," Brian said, "Especially this time of year."

"I know you do."

"You want me to come and hang out for awhile before heading home?"

Her smile answered his question as the bus rounded the corner and stopped at the only bus stop they had ever known. As they headed toward Teagan's house, she looked back over her shoulder and sighed.

Brian nudged her with his elbow. "Hey, I know it's tough that she lived so close and her house is always within sight. But you've held it together better than most. I can't believe she's been gone three years now."

She walked slower and her lips trembled a bit. "Sometimes I'm still so angry at her. We were the three musketeers."

"I know, Teags. It sucks."

They walked in silence up the driveway where Teagan unlocked the door to the sun porch. Brian dumped his bag inside the door and helped her in the kitchen, getting plates and mugs as she opened the refrigerator and took out a chocolate cake and a container of iced coffee.

"Hmm, hmm," Brian sang. "Hel-lo therapy."

"You got that right. Nothing like coffee and chocolate to make a day better."

Teagan cut two big pieces of cake and they sat down at the table. She took a forkful and let it sit on her tongue, closing her eyes to taste the chocolate mingled with a sip of coffee.

"God, I love mocha. There's no better flavor in the world."

Brian nodded in agreement, his mouth full with cake and coffee. He swallowed and took a swig of coffee, wiping his mouth on his sleeve. "Okay, I think you need to talk about it. Joanne's been on your mind all day. What's going on? Is it just the anniversary coming up, or what?"

Teagan looked pensive as she sipped her coffee.

"Not just the anniversary. It's the damn audition announcement today. It brings it all back, you know? It's bad enough that she died, but she took theater with her. I can't imagine doing a show without her, and I miss that. I miss us."

I think you're still pissed off that she made you promise to audition for other shows and make new friends."

"That's a little harsh."

"Look, you've worked through so much grief the past three years – we both have – but I think it's time. It's just gonna eat away at you if you don't."

She savored each bite as he spoke, glad that he understood. Cake couldn't bring Joanne back, but it sure helped her talk about it. "You know what's ironic?", she said. "Cake is like therapy for us, and it was like poison to her. She couldn't even let herself have a friggin' piece of birthday cake in the end. We should have been able to save her."

Brian shook his head. "That's crap and you know it. We *did* try to save her – over and over again. She was just full of excuses and major denial. You can't keep blaming yourself."

"But why the hell did she have to give up? She had so much going for her. Family and friends that loved her, a sister that adored her, and more talent that I'll ever have. Such a big waste. It's just not fair."

"Anorexia's never fair. It sucks."

Teagan sighed. "That last visit was so hard. I think we both knew she was saying good bye, and I just couldn't face the fact that she wouldn't be a part of my life anymore."

Brian cut another slice of cake and put it in front of her. "Look, since she died I've watched you dig yourself out of your grief. You got that job at Caldwell Manor and it's helped to bring you back from the edge. And for the past couple of years you've been doing okay until November rolls around, and then you get bombarded with the anniversary and her birthday – and auditions. I think it's time to deal with that promise so you can move on."

Teagan sat quietly, listening to him. She knew he was right. That first year right after Joanne died there was no way that she could have tried out for anything, let alone the 8th grade musical. But now, in her junior year, she knew she only had two more chances to keep her word, and Brian was right. It was time.

"Okay, I'll do it. That way if I don't make it I can try again next year."

"Hallelujah! It's about time! And this crap about you not getting in – that doesn't sound like you. You might not have danced for a couple of years, but you've still got it, girl."

Teagan laughed as she got up to clear the dishes. She picked up the plates and danced her way to the sink, swaying her big hips from side to side. "You sayin' my dancin' is rusty?"

"Damn girl, if I wasn't gay I'd be hitting on ya right now." He got up and twirled her around.

She laughed, her green eyes smiling at him. "As if that would get you anywhere with my ace ass." She hugged him and added, "But thanks for helping me get to this point. I never would have made it without you."

"Honey, it's the cake……nothing like cake to clear your head and make you smile." He grabbed a towel and dried the plates and mugs as she washed them.

The back door opened and Peg O'Sullivan came in carrying a bag of groceries.

"Momma O! Let me take that," he said, putting the towel down. "How are ya?"

Teagan's mom gratefully handed him the bag as she replied, "Doing okay. Always good to walk in and see you here." She hugged him and then turned to Teagan as she removed her coat. "Hi honey – thanks for doing those." She turned back to Brian

"Did you want to stay for dinner? Nothing fancy, just fajitas tonight."

Brian helped her to unpack the groceries as he replied, "Hmm-mm…..sounds wonderful. But my mom and I had already planned to have dinner tonight. She's stopping at Gino's after work to pick up a calzone for us."

Teagan hung up the towel he had left on the counter. "God, Gino's has the best calzones in the world. Good thing I love fajitas so much or I'd be heading to your house."

Brian looked at the clock. "Hey, I'd best be getting home. I have to work all weekend so I wanna get some homework done tonight. Momma, I'll catch those fajitas next time – and I'll bring a Mexican dessert." He picked up his backpack and turned to Teagan.

"And I'll see you Monday at school, and we can talk more about that audition. And maybe next weekend we can sit and watch the movie to get a better idea of the show. See ya!" He gave them both a quick hug and headed out, and Teagan turned back as her mom got out the cutting board and a knife.

"What's this about an audition?" she asked.

"I decided it was finally time. I'm gonna try out for the show this year."

Peg O'Sullivan put her knife down and gave Teagan a long hug, whispering in her ear, "She's up there listening, and she's so happy to finally hear that you're ready."

Teagan's eyes brimmed with tears. "I hope so, mom. I know I have to keep this promise or I'm never gonna be able to put it behind me." Her voice cracked a bit. "It should have been *her* getting ready. She would have had a major lead this year if she was still here."

Her mom put her finger under Teagan's chin, lifting her face to look directly at her. "Honey, I am so proud of you. And no one is prouder than Joanne. Now, why don't you go and get a start on your homework while I get dinner going. Your Dad will be home soon and I know he'll want to hear all about it at dinner."

"Thanks, mom," Teagan replied. "Love you." She picked up her bag and headed to her room, feeling more upbeat than she had all day.

CHAPTER 2

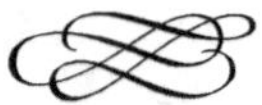

*I*t was Sunday, and sounds of Mitch Miller music filled the activity room at Caldwell Manor Nursing Home. Teagan sang along to every song, moving from one resident to the next as she handed them each an instrument to play.

"Here you go, Kitty," she said to the tall silver haired lady wearing a dress that matched her turquoise eyes. "I know you love the maracas".

Kitty grabbed them, holding them over her head and dancing in her seat. "Oh, I *do*, Miss Teagan! They make me want to shake my hips and flirt with every man in the room!"

Teagan laughed, wondering what that feeling was like. She moved on to the next lady sitting straight and still with her hands in her lap, quietly tapping her toes to the music as she glanced at Kitty with a bit of disdain. The flirt and the prude – what a pair to room together, and yet they seemed to get along well despite their polar personalities.

"Here you go, Gladys," she said as she handed her a small bell. "I know you like the quieter instruments."

"Thank you, Teagan. Someone has to keep her in line." Gladys tried to sound serious, but her mouth slid into a quiet smile as she spoke. "Thank God it's Sunday and it's just Mitch Miller. You should see her on Fridays at Happy Hour when they put on the crooners. My Lord, the woman goes crazy then."

Kitty laughed and gave her roommate a hug. "Honey, I'm old, but I'm not dead! And when Bing or Frank starts to sing, I can't be held responsible for my actions."

Teagan laughed, moving on the smiling gentleman who was listening. "Don't believe a word of it," he said with a wink. "She's all talk and no action!"

"Here you go, Melvin" she said with a chuckle. "You can have the drum today. And I can't fault anyone for being all talk and no action -- makes total sense to me." And she winked back at him.

Melvin laughed. "Oh, Miss Teagan, if I was fifty years younger I'd be trying to change your mind!"

She lovingly tapped his nose with her finger. "And you'd get just as far as you do with Miss Kitty! Now play me some music, you casanova!"

She headed back to the cabinet with the extra instruments. She had come to love her job as an activity aide, and the music groups were her favorite. She had grown up with the music of the older generations, and felt more at home with Mitch Miller and broadway tunes than she ever would with the music of her peers.

It was then that she noticed the new resident, sitting off toward the back of the room in a wheelchair, surveying the group and clearly enjoying the music, but keeping a safe distance away. She approached her with a smile.

"Hi! My name is Teagan, and I work here a few days a week. I know that you must be new here, and sense that maybe you like to warm up to people slowly instead of jumping right into this crazy crew."

The woman in the wheelchair smiled. She had an olive complexion and dark hair pulled back in a bun. The wrinkles around her eyes seemed to dance when she smiled, and Teagan got the feeling that this woman liked to laugh.

"You are quite astute, my dear," the woman replied, extending her hand to Teagan, "My name is Ida Vassilikas, and I just moved in on Friday."

Teagan shook her hand and welcomed her to Caldwell Manor with a smile. "Vassilikas – Greek?" she asked.

Ida nodded. "I was born on the Isle of Crete. My parents were both born and raised there, and even named me after Mt. Ida – which is reportedly where they fell in love."

"Mt. Ida.......isn't there a cave there where Zeus was supposedly born?"

Ida smiled at Teagan and gave a look of approval with her eyes. "You ARE astute, aren't you? I think I'm going to like you, Miss Teagan......" Her voice halted as she waited for the reply.

"O'Sullivan. My parents both have Irish ancestors, but they grew up here in the Caldwell area. My mom always said that this was the town she wanted to live in when they got married and had a family. As soon as they knew I was on the way my dad bought the house I've lived in all my life."

As if on cue, the song "When Irish Eyes Are Smiling" came on, and all the residents called for Teagan. "Sing! Miss Teagan, you gotta sing!"

Ida smiled. "You are evidently a well loved young lady. Go – your audience is calling." Teagan patted her hand and headed back to the middle of the room, singing away as she conducted the residents. They all sang along quite loudly and almost drowned out the CD with their percussion instruments.

She loved them all so much. Their acceptance of her when she started working was a key factor in her dealing with Joanne's death. As weeks past she found solace in their company, and their love of music reignited her passion for singing and performing. Whenever she was having a bad day they'd tell her a story about years gone by and she'd regain perspective about getting through life's trials. Aside from Brian, they had become her best friends.

As she sang, she saw her boss Karen Drake return from a meeting, and noted with satisfaction that Ida had gestured to Karen to move her a little closer to the group. In no time at all they were singing the last song on the CD.

"Okay, all of you! It's time to turn in those instruments and rest your hands and voices. Since we're almost done, how would like me to put on a Lawrence Welk DVD?" Cheers told her the suggestion was well received, and before long Teagan and Karen had everyone's chairs facing the TV screen and watching intently. Teagan made her way back to Ida, who said she'd be heading back to her room shortly.

"I'm still adjusting to the new place, and I'm pretty tired from my granddaughter's visit this morning. I think I'm going to head back and rest."

"Your granddaughter came? How nice for you! Is your family local?"

Ida shook her head. "Until recently, they've been all over. They've actually lived in Houston the past several years, but when I started having problems falling my son-in-law took a job here in Massachusetts so that my daughter could be closer. I'm sure I won't see them TOO often – they're all busy people – but I'll take what I can get."

As she spoke a young woman approached the two of them.

"Ida, it's good to see you out and about. And I see you've met our favorite activity aide."

Teagan smiled. "Aw, Maggie, that's sweet of you to say." She turned to Ida and added, "and Maggie is everyone's favorite social worker."

"Everyone I've met since I arrived has been so kind. But right now I'm getting a little tired, and I think I'd like to head back to my room to rest before dinner."

Maggie patted her shoulder. "I'd be happy to take you back. I'd like to chat with you a few minutes anyway to see if there's any concerns or issues you've had in your first few days."

"That would be appreciated," Ida replied. She turned toward Teagan and added, "It was a delight to meet such a beautiful young woman with an equally lovely name. I look forward to seeing you again."

Teagan smiled at her warmly. "I look forward to that as well, Ida. I'd love to hear more about Crete and your childhood." She waved as

Maggie wheeled Ida out of the room. Charlotte Hurd, the head nurse on duty happened by as Ida and Maggie were leaving.

"She's a nice lady. Arrived from Brentwood on Friday. Her daughter's family is staying at her house. Up from Texas, I think."

"Yeah, she mentioned Houston. I'm glad that she has a family close by. It will help a lot if they visit regularly."

"Let's hope they do. So many don't."

"Well, Ida said that her granddaughter was here earlier today, so that's encouraging."

Charlotte snickered. "Oh, yeah. She was here for about 10 minutes and had her cell phone in front of her most of the visit. Ida sat there with her hands in her lap just studying her. I think they said three sentences to each other and then she was off. Now you know I don't like to judge, but that one didn't rate in my book. Then again, I usually use you to set the bar, and that's a mighty high bar."

Teagan sighed. "Sometimes I feel like I was born in the wrong era. I don't seem to fit in anywhere anymore. It was so much easier back when…." Her voice trailed off as memories welled up inside.

"Back when your best friend was still alive?" Charlotte instinctively gave Teagan a hug. "Now sit and chat with me for a few minutes. My feet are killing me."

They both grabbed a chair at one of the activity tables, and Charlotte continued. "Honey, you started working here a year after Joanne died, and you were madder than hell back then. Some days I was afraid you might not work out as you never seemed to smile."

"I remember. Kitty used to tell me to stop being like Gladys. They were the ones that taught me how to laugh again."

"Yeah, they do that. Point is, once you started opening up you were able to work through so much of the grief process. Hell, you're more together than half of my staff here. Losing a friend – whether by death, or a move, or even a big fight – it still hurts and leaves you alone. So be gentle with yourself."

"Sometimes," Teagan began haltingly, "sometimes I still blame myself for not being able to reach her. And I wonder if my being fat didn't fuel her disease faster."

Charlotte's expression turned serious. "Sometimes those with anorexia do avoid being around fat people, but you'd been friends all your life. Her body image was all screwed up, but I don't think your weight was a big factor."

"I just wish I could have saved her."

"And that's normal. But people with anorexia can't be helped unless they accept their condition and are open to change. It's a tough road to recovery, and it's a life long battle. Don't beat yourself up because you couldn't get Joanne to that place."

Before Teagan could reply they were interrupted by Maggie's return.

"Charlotte, I'm sorry to bug you, but Mona Johnson's daughter is here to finish up the paperwork for her move tomorrow. I need you to go over her medication schedule if that's okay."

Charlotte nodded. "Absolutely. You can start with her and I'll be down in ten minutes."

"Will do. And sorry again for bothering both of you during a break. See ya, Teagan."

She headed out of the activity room and Charlotte turned back toward Teagan. "Now where were we?"

"You were sharing wisdom – like you always do," Teagan replied. "You always seem to know when I begin doubting myself about Joanne's death."

"Honey, you can't blame yourself. Joanne tried, but in the end her disease won out."

Teagan smiled weakly. "You've helped me so much the past couple of years. You and this crazy crew of residents. Talk about feeling loved and accepted."

"They *do* get under our skin, don't they? And a few really do seem to know just what we need some days."

"Exactly. I wish that I could find another person *my* age that does. High school's a big game where everybody judges everybody else on their looks, their size, the music they like, and what they do on their weekends. It all seems so fake. And the whole dating thing? I just don't get it. And I never will."

"I suspect there are others out there who are also lonely and unsure of themselves," Charlotte responded, "but they aren't as outspoken as you are, so they adapt by wearing a mask to fit in. You – you're genuine and direct and don't play games."

"Unless it's bingo here on a Sunday afternoon," Teagan replied with a smirk.

Charlotte chuckled. "Seriously, though, your candor is a strength in today's world, and there are kids out there that really want to find that. So don't give up on finding another friend like Joanne – she's out there, but you gotta find her and help her get rid of the mask."

Charlotte looked at her watch, and reached out to squeeze Teagan's hand.

"Well, my dear, break time is over, and your shift is about done. I do love our chats, though. You're like the daughter I never had."

"Thanks, Charlotte. You're like a second mom to me, but I suspect that the real one is out in the car waiting to pick me up, so I'd best get going. Thanks for always knowing what to say."

CHAPTER 3

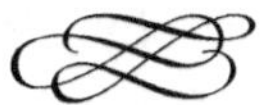

The following Friday afternoon Teagan left high school with Brian and walked the short distance to the library where Brian worked as a page. As he greeted his coworkers she found her favorite table off toward the end of the reference section. She had a good view of the circulation desk and the adult stacks, but most of the library traffic headed away from her spot. Aside from home, it was her favorite place to study.

She stared at her assignment for health class, and while she had chosen her topic already, she was wondering if another would have been less stressful. Teagan had been excited when the assignment was first announced, as she loved writing research papers. However, the presentation *also* included an oral presentation after the papers were completed; to make matters worse, the teacher was to pair up students to share their own papers with each other and then work together on a presentation for the class.

Teagan had originally thought of exploring the topic of body positivity and being healthy at any weight, and still loved the idea of trying to make a difference and educate those with prejudices against fat people. She also briefly considered the topic of asexuality, but wasn't sure if she was ready to open up about her own story. And while the idea of sharing with the class was a little intimidating, the prospect of working closely with someone else beforehand was a lot worse. She concluded that a different topic would be easier. Like venereal disease, or meningitis.

In the end, she had decided on the topic of anorexia. Many of her peers had been in her class when Joanne died, and she remembered some of the shock and sorrow that was expressed. No one ever expected that Joanne might actually die from her eating disorder – especially not in middle school. Counselors had come in to talk to the kids about what had happened, but there wasn't any long term support. Teagan and Brian had gone to counseling weekly after that, but aside from a few others at the dance studio there weren't many kids that had been that close to Joanne.

Over time, lunchtime conversations about diets and nutrition were replaced by sports, movies, and who liked who. Teagan and Brian became closer as they ate lunch together daily, but as a result they became more distant from their classmates. It took a lot longer for them to get over blaming themselves for nagging Joanne about how little she ate or how obsessed with calories she was. She had even gotten permission from Joanne's family to openly discuss what had happened. Even though sharing it all would be painful, Teagan felt that she was finally strong enough to talk about it with others – especially if it might help them in recognizing the symptoms of anorexia and how best to respond to them.

Brian sauntered by carrying a few magazines that needed to be shelved. "Hey, Teags, guess what movie the library has?"

She looked up and waited expectantly for him to continue.

"They have 'Kiss Me Kate' in. I thought I could put it aside and we could watch it tonight. You game?"

Teagan nodded in agreement, and Brian smiled and headed off.

"*So,*" she thought to herself, "*it looks like I really AM going through with this.*"

All of a sudden the research paper became a great distraction, if only to not have to think about the promise of the upcoming audition. She spent the next couple of hours jotting down notes and drafting a basic outline and then explored the library catalog to see what resources were available for research.

Teagan had called her mom before Brian got off of work and gotten permission to head home with him. One of the great things about living in Caldwell was that everything in town was close enough to walk to. She grabbed her bag as Brian came out of the library office and they headed out into the cool, crisp air.

"Wanna hit Gino's for pizza?" Brian asked as they crossed the street and headed down Main Street. Leaves rustled by in the fall breezes, and Teagan loved hearing them crunch as they walked.

"Considering that pizza is my favorite food in the world, AND that Gino's has the best pizza ever, that's a no-brainer. Do you wanna eat there or get it to go?"

"Let's get it to go – then we can eat it as we watch the movie."

She nodded. "I love it when a plan comes together."

Brian grinned, recognizing the reference to the A-Team, one of their favorite old TV shows. He told her about his shift as they walked the two blocks to Gino's and pulled open the door. A little bell signaled their arrival, and the scents of mozzarella, garlic, and tomato wafted through the air to greet them.

"God, I love this place," said Teagan. "I may be Irish, but my stomach must be Italian."

Gino was behind the counter just finishing up a phone order. He smiled at them as he hung up the phone. "Buena sera! How are two of my favorite people?"

"We're hungry, Gino!" replied Brian. "Can we have a large pizza with sausage, onion, and pepper to go?"

"What? You're not staying tonight? It breaks my heart. I love having the young people come in to eat. I'd give you your favorite table – nice and romantic!"

"Next time, Gino, I promise", said Brian. "We have to watch a movie for homework, so gotta take it with us this time."

"That's fine – you sit now and let me work my magic."

They both chuckled as they sat in the chairs designated for take out orders. Gino would forever think they were a couple, and at this point they stopped trying to explain things to him. Easier to just let him dote on them and give them advice on love and long lasting relationships. They loved watching his Italian hands fly around as he spoke from the heart. Gino was forever a romantic and he wanted the whole world to join him.

The bell jingled again as the door opened and a cold blast of air blew in. An old man entered, all bundled up in a tattered coat with a scarf around his neck. He removed his gloves as he made his way to the counter.

Gino smiled as he grabbed a brown bag sitting on the counter. "Buena serra, Mr. Pritchard. Good to see you again."

"What's so good about it? Blasted weather. It's gettin' cold way too early."

Gino nodded in agreement. "We can't control Mother Nature, now can we? That'll be $14.99 for your lasagna and breadsticks. It'll be a nice hot meal on such a chilly night."

The old man handed him a twenty and waited for his change. "I hope so. It better not be too spicy. Last time I was up half the night from all that garlic." He stuck his change in his pocket and put his gloves back on before taking his meal from Gino.

"Garlic is good for you, my friend. But since you mentioned it when you called your order in, I stuck a free biscotti in your bag. A peace offering from your friend Gino."

Mr. Pritchard scowled as he headed back out the door, cursing quietly as the cold air hit him. Gino watched him go, and then smiled at Teagan and Brian. "That old curmudgeon. He complains about every little thing, but he keeps coming back." He chuckled as he turned back toward his work.

Brian laughed. "Old man Pritchard really is the town curmudgeon, isn't he? God, he's been grouchy my whole life. Gino's a saint for listening to him complain every time he walks in the door. He must not hate the food that much if he keeps buying it."

"My folks said that he used to eat here every Friday night with his wife when she was still alive. It was like their date night. He still comes in every Friday night for takeout. No wonder Gino loves him. Hey, should we add in some biscotti for dessert?"

"Nope, not tonight! I made a new dessert last night, and you can be my number two guinea pig. My mom had some last night and as far as I know she's still alive and well."

"As if you could ever make anything that wasn't delicious. So what it is, or are ya gonna surprise me?"

"A new cookie, Teags. Recipe is from Australia. They're called Anzac biscuits.

"What's in them?"

"Rolled oats are the main ingredient, along with butter and a little coconut," Brian responded. He was happy to see her smile with approval. Baking was his favorite thing to do, and Teagan was always happy to sample his new recipes.

"They sound wonderful – although it's kind of a weird name."

"The Anzac stands for Australia and New Zealand Army Corp. and they were popular during World War I. Wives used to send them to their soldiers as they didn't spoil too fast.

Gino signaled that their pizza was ready, and after paying they headed for the door.

"Buono notte!" Gino yelled after them. "You two come again soon!"

"Ciao, Gino!" Teagan called back. "We will! Thanks for the pizza!"

They headed west on Center Street and walked briskly through the scattered leaves. It got dark early in November and the air got cold as soon as the sun went down. Teagan loved this time of year more than any other, and she hopped from side to side along the side-walk to find leaves to walk though.

They turned left onto School Street where Brian's apartment building took up the short block. The lights in the window signaled that Brian's mom had gotten home ahead of them, and she greeted them both warmly as they entered.

"Hi, Mom! We're home! And we have food!"

Terry Morris took the pizza from her son and gave him a quick kiss on the cheek. She smiled at Teagan and said, "Let me put this down so I can give you a proper hug." They followed her to the kitchen where Terry had plates waiting on the counter next to a bowl of salad. She gave Teagan the promised hug and handed her a plate.

"Eat – the two of you! I'll put on some music while you're getting your pizza."

"You gonna join us for dinner, mom? It's movie night with Kiss Me Kate."

"I'll have some pizza and salad with you, but I think I'll leave the movie to the two of you and retreat to a warm bed. I'm halfway through a Stephen King novel and he beats out Shakespeare for me."

Teagan laughed. "Better you than I, Mrs. Morris……there are few that can beat out Shakespeare in my book."

As they loaded their plates, the soundtrack from Hamilton the Musical filled the room. Both Teagan and Brian began singing at the top of their lungs. Teagan used her fork as a microphone and turned to Brian. "I will forever be in your debt for getting me hooked on this musical."

Brian grinned as even his mom sang along. They sat at the small dining table and had dinner, and afterwards Teagan helped to clear the dishes while Brian got the movie out.

"I can drive you home later if you want, Teagan," Terry said, "Just let me know."

"It's only two blocks. And you know how much I love walking in the cold."

"Well, the offer stands if you change you mind. Enjoy your movie."

"You want some Anzac biscuits later on, Mom?" Brian asked. "I can bring some in to you if do."

"Don't worry about me," she replied, giving him a quick kiss good-night. "If I get hungry later on I'll come out to get a few. Night, Teagan."

"Night, Mrs. Morris – enjoy your date with Stephen King."

Terry chuckled as she headed down the short hallway and disappeared.

Brian loaded the movie into the DVD player while Teagan turned off their dinner music. "Sorry, Hamilton, but Shakespeare beckons," she whispered as she hit the stop button. She and Brian curled up on opposite ends of the couch, each grabbing blankets to cuddle up in. As the overture began, Brian spoke.

"So, how much do you know about the show, Teags?"

She settled in to the warmth of her blanket as she replied, "I know it's based on Shakespeare's 'Taming of the Shrew', and that it's a story within a story, but beyond that I'm not too familiar with it. And I have NO idea what parts there are – which doesn't really matter. I figure I'll just be trying out for the ensemble anyway."

"Seriously? The ensemble?"

"Yes, seriously. I'm keeping my promise and trying out. But Joanne was the one that got the big leads – not her fat friend. Besides, it's been awhile. I think the ensemble will be a good way to get back into theater."

Brian hit the play button instead of giving a quick synopsis, deciding to let the story tell itself. They watched the first act, laughing and commenting on the various roles and plot points. Brian hit the pause button so they could have they own intermission. He brought mugs of coffee and Anzac biscuits for Teagan to try.

She took a bite and let the crunchy sweetness of oats, butter, and coconut mingle in her mouth.

"Oh, my God, Brian, these are wonderful!" She took another bite. "Maple syrup? Is that the extra sweetness I'm tasting?"

Brian nodded with satisfaction. "So, here's my latest project. For Geography this year I'm doing an extra credit year-long assignment for an extra half credit. Mr. Burton is letting me choose a baked item for each area we study this year and research the history and cultural background of the food, and then bring it in for the class to try. I'm really excited about it, and I have recipes for Thailand, Japan, and Russia all lined up already."

Teagan listened intently as she munched on her biscuit. "Almost wish I had taken geography now.....but I volunteer to taste test every recipe before you bring it in."

"Duh! That's a given. So, changing the subject back to our homework, what parts do you think I should try for? I don't think I'd want the lead, but maybe one of Bianca's suitors might be fun. Or Paul, Fred's assistant. Or maybe even one of the gangsters. What do you think?"

Teagan patted the couch cushion. "I think," she started, "that we should shut up and watch the rest of the movie to figure all that out."

He laughed as he grabbed the remote.

"That's one of the reasons I love you, Teags – you're always so sensible."

With that they turned their attention to the Entracte and Act Two. Brian offered to walk her home afterwards, so they bundled up and headed out into the cold night air for the short walk up School Street.

"Brrrr!" Brian said, pulling his scarf around his neck. "Starting to really get cold at night now."

"Hmmm, yes is it," Teagan replied, "and I LOVE it!" She gave a little leap and did a twirl as they walked.

"Going for a dancing part, are we?" he joked.

"Hell no -- I haven't danced in three years. I doubt very much I'd be in the running for a major part. I kind of liked the role of Hattie. She has that little solo at the beginning, and maybe I could handle a small supporting role. I think I could even handle the bit of dancing that she does with the ensemble."

"Hey, I could see you there," Brian said. "And if I ended with the role of Paul we could dance together."

He grabbed her by the waist and twirled her around.

Teagan's laugh filled the air. "Then we'd better not let Gino come to the show or he'd have us married off by the end of the it!"

Brian stopped her and looked serious. "But why aren't you considering going out for the lead? Can't you see yourself as Kate, spewing insults and throwing things at Petruchio? It's like the perfect role for my little aro/ace buddy."

Teagan stepped back. "The lead? Are you crazy? I haven't done anything on stage since 7th grade. I couldn't handle that part."

"That's crap, Teags. You perform three times a week at Caldwell Manor. The residents LOVE you, and they eat it up when you turn on your theatrical charm."

"But there's a huge difference between hamming it up at work and being the lead."

"What would Joanne be telling you right now?"

"That's not fair. Joanne's not exactly here now, is she?" Teagan walked on ahead, clearly in a huff.

Brian quickened his step to catch up. "I'm just saying that she wouldn't want you to come back as a wimp. That's not your style and you know it."

Teagan kept quiet as they turned on to Monroe Drive, considering Brian's words. "I hate it when you're right. Okay, so maybe the role of Kate might be fun. But that person is also the part of Lilli, who does all that romantic stuff with Fred. There's no way I could make that stuff believable."

Brian bumped her shoulder with his. "It's called ACTING."

They'd reached Teagan's driveway, and she stopped to give him a goodnight hug.

He smiled at her. "At least *think* about it...you'd get to sing all about hating men..."

She smirked as she headed toward the door, but turned back just before going inside.

"Night, Brian – thanks for walking me home. And I'll take it under advisement."

She headed in, and Brian turned for home, laughing to himself as he pictured her on the stage throwing props around at all the guys. It really was the perfect role for his best friend.

CHAPTER 4

The sun was bright and the air was crisp on Sunday afternoon, and Teagan decided to ride her bike to work. Even as a fat teen she loved riding her bike around town, and over time she learned to ignore the scowls and pointed fingers at the fat girl riding her bike. As she approached the corner of Monroe Drive she looked across Washington Street and saw kids playing at the park by the Elementary School. She watched a young chubby girl climbing the jungle gym with her braids flying around behind her, laughing up at the sun. Teagan remembered doing the same thing at about the same age. As she stopped to catch her breath, she observed two other girls near the jungle gym, laughing and gesturing toward the one now sitting near the top. Teagan didn't need to hear everything to know that they were taunting her because of her weight. She remembered the sting of words, and the shame that so often followed. As she got older, she came to realize the power of society's prejudices and was determined not to let anyone define her by her weight. Some days were harder than others, but most of the time she stayed positive.

"*You go, little girl,*" she said to herself as she watched the youngster. "*Don't let anyone make you feel inferior. Show the world – or at least our little town – how to live life to the fullest.*"

She had loved growing up in Caldwell. Living in a small town felt like extended family. She had lived in the same house on Monroe Drive all her life, and walked up to this very corner every day when her mom walked her to school. As she got older, she moved further up School Street to the Middle School, nestled right behind Caldwell Elementary. It wasn't until high school that she started taking a bus, and even then she could manage the walk if she wanted to.

She turned right onto Washington Street and headed over the creek. The north end of Main Street went off to her right, and across the street to her left Caldwell Cemetery sprawled from the creek to the church at the far end. Throughout the cemetery small stone benches were placed for visitors to sit and meditate or pray. Up until Joanne's death three years earlier, the two of them would often ride their bikes to the cemetery on a Sunday afternoon. They loved reading the different stones and seeing the etchings that gave hints to those laid to rest. At times they would sit on a bench and make up whole life stories about who each person was and how they met their demise. Joanne had always said that the cemetery was one of the most peaceful places in town.

"Well, it WAS," Teagan thought as she rode by. All that changed the day she stood toward the back of the cemetery, her eyes glued to the mahogany casket before her. *"People aren't supposed to die in the 8th grade,"* she thought. A month later a beautiful marble stone was placed to stand guard over Joanne. Along the sides of the stone were ivy leaves intertwined with music notes, and a small white marble angel perched on top, her hands folded in prayer as she looked down. It was like having an angel literally praying over Joanne for eternity. *"Would've been nice if the angel had been watching over her BEFORE then,"* thought Teagan as she pedaled past.

As Teagan rode by she could see Mr. Pritchard, affectionately named 'the old curmudgeon" by most people in town, sitting on one of the benches near the front of the cemetery. If it was Sunday, most townspeople who passed by knew that they'd see him sitting by his wife's grave. *"He must have really loved her to be here so often,"* thought Teagan. *"I wonder how she put up with such a grouchy old man?"*

Looking past Mr. Pritchard, Teagan spotted a thin girl around her age jogging toward the back of the cemetery. Joanne would have been there next to her if she were still alive. She passed the church on the left and town hall on the right, and gave thanks that this stretch of the ride was all flat. It made it easier to bike around town without getting winded. Caldwell Manor stood back from the road at the corner with two big maple trees adorning the front walkway. Right now the lawn was blanketed in yellow leaves as most of the foliage had fallen, and if Teagan wasn't heading in to work she might have jumped off her bike just to wade through them. God, how she loved autumn!

She rode her bike around to the back and entered through the garden patio area. Several patients were sitting outside enjoying the sunshine. Kitty was sitting with family members when she spotted Teagan, and waved her arm invitingly.

"Teagan, come and say hi to my grandson!" Teagan smiled and walked over to where Kitty sat with her daughter and grandson, who was about 4-5 years old. He was constantly moving every time he came to visit, and today was no exception.

"I remember Max," she said as the young blond boy stopped to look at her as he played with the dirt around the fall mums.

"You're the big, fat, drum lady!" he beamed. "Can I play the drum?"

Both Kitty and her daughter gasped, and Kitty scolded, "Maxwell, that's not nice!"

Teagan laughed. There was a time when she was younger when the name calling got under her skin, but she learned along the way to love herself for who she was. "That's okay, Kitty.....I *am* a big, fat drum lady, and kids at this age are just stating what they see – there's no malicious meaning or judgement attached." She turned to Max, who had already turned back to his flower and dirt. "Max, maybe next time you come you can play the drum. Right now I have to go and run a bingo game."

"Bingo!" Max yelled. "I LOVE bingo!" He proceeded to sing at the top of lungs "B-I-N-G-O, B-I-N-G-O......" as Teagan greeted Kitty's daughter and then headed inside.

Karen Drake was off today, so she was in charge of activities on her own. She had a bingo game scheduled, which was always well attended, and then a short trivia game before ending with a video about the crooners of the 30s and 40s. The afternoon promised to fly by quickly. As she entered the activity room many residents were already in their seats waiting for her. Gladys was standing by the storage closet ready to hand out bingo cards – a job she insisted on doing every week.

"Hi, Gladys," Teagan said. "I don't know what I'd do without you! You could probably run bingo by yourself!"

Gladys shook her finger at Teagan as the closet was opened. "Oh, no, you're not going to get me up at that table calling numbers. Then I wouldn't be able to play my lucky cards!"

Teagan laughed as she handed Gladys the cards, watching her head to her right to place bingo cards in front of everyone. If a seat was still empty she left one card in place in case someone arrived late and still wanted to play. Every now and then Teagan saw her move the card at the top of the pile and place it at the bottom. She chuckled, knowing that those were Gladys' "lucky" cards, and probably the motivation for her weekly chore.

Teagan set up the bingo cage and put all the balls inside, and then waited a few more minutes before starting. God forbid she started before 1:30. Bingo was one of the most popular events of the week, and sometimes even a visiting relative joined in. She wondered if Kitty would be arriving with Max in tow. He could be a bit of a hand-ful, but sometimes letting him call out the numbers kept him busy until he got bored, and then he'd sit and play with a handful of bingo markers next to his grandmother, often spotting the number on the card for her and pointing at it loudly.

Teagan looked around to see if Ida Vassilikas had decided to attend, and was a little disappointed not to see her. Although she was settling in nicely, Teagan could tell that some activities were more favored that others, and bingo did not seem high on the list. She hoped to find her at some point during the day to check in on her. The residents made her aware that it was now 1:30 and time to start. Just as bingo couldn't start early, it better not start late, either.

An hour later, Gladys helped her put the cards away as Melvin carefully placed all the balls back into the coffee can used for storage. These two, along with Kitty, were her favorite residents, and she never turned down their help. Of the three, only Kitty's family visited, and she often felt bad for these two who had only their peers and staff to call "family."

"Here you go, Miss Teagan," Melvin reported as he handed her the coffee can. "All numbers accounted for! I'll get you the cage, too." He returned to the table to get the cage, and warmly scolded Gladys who was still working. "Come on, lady! We don't got all day! It's trivia time and I want a good seat!"

Gladys just scowled at him and continued around the tables, methodically picking up each card and placing it on the pile. Teagan zipped around the room gathering all the bingo markers, and before long the closet was locked and they were heading down to the parlor where Sunday trivia was held. It had been her suggestion last year to move it from the activity room. She had noticed that staying in one place all afternoon resulted in many residents nodding off during trivia, but giving them a little time to move to another location kept them awake and alert. Some residents headed back to their rooms for a Sunday nap or visit, and others arrived for trivia having skipped bingo. Teagan was glad to see that Ida was part of that second group.

She sat in her wheelchair next to the blue upholstered wingback chair designated for the activity leader and smiled as Teagan approached.. "Ida!" she exlaimed, "I'm so glad that you came to join us! Trivia is one of my favorite activities and I thought you might like a couple of today's questions."

Ida smiled and tapped the side of her head with her finger. "I have to keep this part of my body sharp at least – the rest might not work as well, but my mind still chugs along at top speed!"

Teagan chuckled as Melvin settled in to a seat on Ida's other side. "It better be chuggin' if you're gonna beat me, lady," he said. "They call me the trivia king around here."

Teagan sat down with her trivia notebook in hand, loving that the chair was roomy enough for her ample frame to relax in. "Okay, guys, today's trivia is broken into two themes, but the questions will be asked randomly. The themes are 'Name that Country' and 'Who Sang this Song?' I'll start with an easy one: Which country is where you'll find the Leaning Tower of Pisa?"

The residents almost yelled out "Italy" in unison. Teagan gave them three more questions on geography before switching to music. "Who sang this song about love in the springtime?" She then went on to start singing the opening bars of "April Love", and several residents yelled out Pat Boone's name. They loved it when she sang them the questions – it was her own version of "Name That Tune", and they sang right along with her when they got the answer. Often there would be a lot of reminiscing that would follow about days gone by.

"Okay, last question of the day – and this is a TOUGH one! Name the country where a mountain sits on an island, and contains a cave where Zeus was reportedly born." She watched as Ida's eyes lit up and gave her a wink.

"That would be Greece!" she yelled out, the wrinkles around her eyes beaming. She looked at Teagan and thanked her without words for remembering their conversation. The others clapped in approval and Melvin reached over to shake her hand. "That was a tough one, and you were the only one that knew it – I guess that makes you the trivia queen today!"

Teagan announced the movie for Sunday "tea time", and residents all waited patiently for Teagan and a couple of other staff to pass out refreshments. Teagan knew that once the DVD started she'd have some time to visit with residents individually, and she hoped that Ida might choose that over the video. Almost on cue, Ida raised her hand to ask for someone to wheel her back to her room.

"I'll take you, Ida", Teagan offered. "Do you want to head back to your room right away, or would you like to sit outside in the sunshine for a little while?" The woman smiled and nodded to her suggestion, and they headed out to the garden area where they were alone. They sat facing the west where the fall sunshine could warm them for at least a little while.

"That was nice of you to include that last question, Miss Teagan –

but I guess I *should* have been disqualified as it was rigged." Her eyes twinkled as she spoke, and she chuckled. "But it was by far my favorite activity so far."

Teagan filed away that fact. "It's always nice to see you laughing and having a good time. You seem to be settling in, although I imagine it's still a huge adjustment after living on your own."

Ida turned toward her, her eyes squinting a bit from the sun. "I thought at first it might be. I lived in a big old house by myself for years, and I've loved my independence all my life. But the past year or so I've fallen several times, and I have to confess that I was getting nervous about being alone. When I started to lose my mobility, my house became more of a prison than a haven – does that make sense?"

Teagan nodded. "It really does. It's one thing to be able to come and go and live your life to the fullest, but not having that ability must be a huge adjustment. Especially if you've been accustomed to it – and I have a feeling that you've always been active."

"That I have," Ida replied. "But it's a new season of life, and I'm enjoying the quieter pace with more time to reflect on things. I'm grateful that Caldwell Manor offers so much to keep me active and busy, but still lets me have time to myself. It's a beautiful place to find that new balance, and I'm quickly learning to call it home."

Teagan marveled at her wisdom and ability to adjust to life's cirmcumstances. "And your old home? Will you be selling it at some point? Will that…..be hard?"

Ida shook her head. "When I left Crete it hurt a lot more – I guess that will always be 'home' in my mind. Over the years I've come to believe that a house is just a place. Yes, it's filled with memories and hopefully some beautiful items to cherish, but in the end it's a building with STUFF. That makes it easier to leave. Right now my daughter and her family are living there, and I had put the house in her name when she was a young adult still at home, so they shouldn't lose it unless they choose to give it up."

"And your daughter's name is….."

"Eliana. A good Greek name. She runs her own business selling those fancy handbags and totes. She pops in a couple of days a week during the morning to have coffee, but she's super busy with the kids later in the day. And Frank likes her home in the evening and on weekends. He works in Boston and gets home late in the day, and weekends he usually works on the house."

"Any kids?" Teagan asked.

Ida nodded. "Two. A granddaughter and a grandson. The younger, Philip, is 13, and Cassandra is a few years older. She was actually here this morning for a short visit. She said she had a lot of studying to do, but I think she just says that to leave as early as she can. She never stays long, but at least she still comes."

"Cassandra – that's a beautiful name. Greek as well?" Teagan asked.

"Absolutely. She's a beautiful young woman. Creative, artistic, and quite the performer. You two would probably hit it off in that area.....but lately I'm a little worried about her."

Teagan leaned it closer. "How so?"

"She's just more ....distant. She doesn't say much anymore. She used to talk her head off whenever we were together, and she'd tell me all about her dreams and plans. I remember back a few years – I believe she was in seventh grade then – and they had come up to visit for the holidays. I took her to see her favorite Broadway show at the Brentwood Playhouse because it was touring. Are you by any chance familiar with *Fiddler on the Roof?*"

"Oh, my God! I was there the same time! It was my best friend's favorite as well, and we couldn't miss it. The dancing was phenomenal."

Ida smiled as she reminisced. "That's just how my Cassandra felt about Fiddler. She talked non stop about it for rest of her visit. Now I'm lucky to hear how her day went. I'm guessing it's just the stress of moving, or maybe that's just how teenagers are now." Ida shivered a bit, and Teagan noticed the sun getting lower in the sky.

"How about we get you back inside before it gets any chillier out here?" Teagan asked as she stood up. "Lord knows you don't have *half* the insulation that I do." She patted her stomach and Ida laughed.

"You, my dear, are a breath of fresh air. There aren't many who are so comfotable with who they are at your age, and it's wonderful to have met you."

"Thanks, Ida," Teagan replied as she opened the door. "The feeling is mutual."

Within a half hour Teagan was heading back out the door to get her bike. The sun was getting lower and she knew she could make it home before dark if she headed that way immediately, but she had one stop that she put off long enough. Within minutes she was turning her bike into the cemetery, and as she spotted the angel statue she realized she wasn't the only one there.

She recognized the Newton's car parked in the distance, and then saw Joanne's mom and younger sister raking leaves and cleaning up the grave. Sometimes Teagan still had trouble admitting that Joanne was gone forever, but it was always glaringly obvious here with her name etched in front of her along with when she was born and when she died. Teagan sighed, the hole in her heart still feeling the void that her best friend left.

Beth, Joanne's sister, saw her first. "Teagan!" She met Teagan when she stopped her bike and threw her arms around her for a hug. "I miss you!" Teagan hugged her back, and then turned for another from Joanne's mother Cheryl. "Hey Momma C – how ya doin'?"

Cheryl held her tight for a moment, and then stepped back to look straight her. "Better now. You always make me feel better. Were you at work?"

Teagan nodded. She turned to Beth and said, "So, kiddo, how are you liking high school so far?" She made a mental note that she needed to spend more time with Beth, who had been like a younger sister for years.

"It's okay. I love English and history – math I could do without, and science is okay." She stopped for a second, and then remembered something else. "Oh, and guess what I'm gonna do?"

Teagan waited expectantly, knowing that Beth would just continue without a reply. "I'm trying out for Kiss Me, Kate! Like, this week!"

For a second, the date of the upcoming audition being so close took Teagan's breath away, and then she remembered the reason for being here in the cemetery today and answered, "That's awesome. And with your talent, I'm sure that you'll get in as a freshman!"

"I hope so. I'm really nervous."

Teagan swallowed hard. "Me, too. I'm trying out, too." There. She'd said it.

Beth threw her arms around her for the second time and hugged hard, jumping up and down. "Really? Oh, God that makes it so much better! Mom, can I sit and the car and text Julie? I wanna tell her."

Cheryl Newton nodded and then turned to Teagan and put her hands on the girl's shoulders. "I was hoping you'd be ready for Beth's first year. I'm proud of you, honey." She eyes filled with tears as she turned her eyes toward the angel on the stone. "She is, too…..probably more than anyone."

Teagan let the tears flow as Joanne's mom held her. She could still hear her best friend's voice – frail and weak instead of belting out in song like she should have been: "Teagan, promise me that you'll still try out for the show. It'll help you find someone else. You're the best friend in the world, and I want someone else to know that, too. Promise me." And Teagan had promised.

Cheryl Newton gave her a squeeze and handed her a tissue. "I knew you couldn't audition that year – we were all devastated. I've been praying that you'd get to the point where you could again. You're so amazing on stage, my dear."

Teagan looked at her, and then the at the angel. "I think I'm finally ready, Momma C. After all, I have a promise to keep."

CHAPTER 5

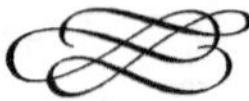

Teagan knew that the day of auditions would be a long one, and she was grateful that it also happened to be Brian's birthday so that she'd have a distraction. They met for lunch outside where a few other peers gathered to enjoy the crisp air and sunshine. Teagan scanned the clusters, recognizing a couple of girls from her AP classes at the other end of the courtyard. They were sitting with a small group of girls at a table next to some guys having an intense conversation about sports. Teagan could tell that while sports might be the conversation at one table, the girls were discussing boys. Occasional glances over their shoulders followed by nods and quiet chatter told the story.

"I will never understand the dating world," Teagan sighed, turning her attention back to Brian. "Just seems like so much wasted energy, and for what?"

Brian flashed a smile, looking past her to the guys having a heated discussion about which wide receiver was the best. "Oh, I can think of a few things, Teags. Hey, you could get me one of *them* for my birthday."

Teagan glanced at the guys and threw a cheese curl at him. "Damn. Had I known *that's* what you wanted I wouldn't have wasted my time in the kitchen last night." She reached into her lunchbox and pulled out a plastic container and handed it over to him with a plastic fork. "Happy birthday – made your favorite."

"Carrot cake? You are the *best*." He opened the container and licked the cream cheese frosting with his tongue. "Ahhh, so good!" as he took a big bite of cake. "This might even make me wonder if cake isn't better than romance."

Teagan took a bite and laughed. "Without a doubt, my friend. Every time."

"You make a damn good cake, Teags. Not gonna lie."

She chuckled. "And who gave me the recipe, Mr. God of the Kitchen?"

He laughed, wiping his mouth on his sleeve.

"That was delicious, even if I *did* tell you how to make it. Maybe *you* should be making the stuff I bring in for geography class."

"Hell, no – you're the cook. I'm just your taste tester," Teagan answered as she finished her cupcake, " Best job in the world, I might add. Your baked goods are so damn delicious. You should go into culinary arts or something."

"Maybe someday……how about a library with coffee and a bakery inside? That would be my dream job."

"You'd make a killing. Believe me. Books and brownies together? With coffee? It's all my favorite things in the world in one place. And I know there's a ton of others who would agree."

"Ready for auditions later on?" Brian asked as he licked his fingers.

She nodded. "Ready as I'll ever be. I'm really nervous after being away from it for three years. How 'bout you?"

Brian stood up and started gathering his stuff. "Honey, I've been waiting to strut my stuff!" He glanced at the clock over the door. "But for now, I get to head off to geography class."

Teagan sighed. "I'd *so* rather be in your class. I get to go to Health class. Yay." She picked up her bookbag, brushed the crumbs off of her sweatshirt, and flashed Brian a smile as they headed in opposite directions. "Meet you outside the auditorium after school."

Health class proved as boring as she thought it would be. Before putting on a video about the danger of fast food, her teacher spoke briefly about their projects.

"Remember, you all have papers due right before Christmas on the topics you selected. But looking ahead, I want you to know that in January, I'll be pairing you up with someone to do a presentation together." Teagan groaned along with several others. God, she hated working on presentations with other people. Someone was asking how that would be possible with everyone doing separate topics. *"Good question,"* thought Teagan, *"maybe he'll change his mind."*

Instead, he explained that over break he would look topics over and match people up as closely as he could. "It'll be up to you to decide how to link the topics."

"Yeah, good luck with that," she thought, *"because most of us will hate whoever you stick us with."* Discussion ended quickly as the movie went on, during which time Teagan doodled in her notebook, trying not to feel guilty about the fact that she loved fast food – even if the narrator was telling her that it was the worst thing in the world to eat. *"Just one more way society is so unfair. When thin people eat fast food they're just seen as making an occasional bad choice, but when us fat people eat the same cheeseburger we're just seen as bad people. No way am I giving up my chicken wings and pizza."*

An hour later she found Brian waiting at the entrance to the auditorium. The butterflies in her stomach were fluttering about for the first time in years, but she thought of Joanne and was determined to go in and give it her best. They walked down the aisle and signed in at the table, picking up an audition packet and filing into the second row of seats. Teagan filled out all the information, hesitating only as she filled in her weight as 220 pounds. She remembered earlier years when she'd lie and put down a lower weight, but as she became more accepting of herself she realized that any costume coordinator would soon discover the deceit anyway. Teagan frowned at how tight a fit the seats were. Her dad had always told her to run for office or become an activist for fat people's rights, and most auditorim seats made her consider it.

As she was finishing up, a girl from her AP History class stood up to speak. "Hey all," she started, "I want to welcome all of you to auditions for Kiss Me, Kate. My name is Ann Kirkland, and I'll be your stage manager – which means that you bug me for anything before bugging Mr. C." She gestured to a middle aged man with dark curly hair; he waved to the group and stepped forward as well.

"Thanks, Ann," he started, "and she's right – always bug her first!" Laughter from the students seem to ease the tension as he continued. "My name is Mr. Calabreshi, but you can call me Mr. C. I've been directing here at the high school for a couple of years, and I'm excited to be starting another production with all of you. The other two ladies that are sitting here are Maureen Kelly, music director, and Liz Patterson, our choreographer. They'll both be working with you shortly, but let me go over the rehearsal schedule with all of you first and answer a few questions."

A short while later he finished up, and proceeded with directions. "Okay, because there are a lot of you, we'll be splitting you into two groups. You all have a number on your packets. All odd numbers will head across the hall with Mrs. Kelly for music auditions, and the even numbers will stay here for a quick dance segment. And don't worry, we're not expecting you all to dance like pros – we'll be looking for some featured dancers, but for the rest of the cast we just need to know that you can move."

Teagan groaned inside when she bid Brian good luck and watched him head out the door, but was at least glad for the chance to stand up and move away from the seats for thin people. She suddenly felt very alone as she headed up onto the stage; she knew a lot of these peers, and she was well liked enough by most of them, but she didn't really hang out with any of them. *"Okay, Joanne,"* she thought to herself, *"give me a sign that you're here to help me through this."*

Almost immediately, she felt someone nudge her from behind. As she turned to see who it was, she grinned to see Beth Newton following her up the stairs.

"Hey! So glad that you didn't change your mind. Good luck!" She gave Teagan's hand a little squeeze and headed off with a friend, but it was enough to give her the confidence she needed.

Liz Patterson, the choreographer, addressed the group. "Okay, there are more of you than can fit on the stage comfortably, so we'll be dancing through the routines in groups. Anyone with more than five years dance experience head to the sides, and I'll teach the easier dance first."

Teagan headed over to the group of more experienced dancers, noting that Beth was in this group as well. She recognized a couple of girls that she had danced with up through middle school, and they waved at her and smiled. She found herself standing next to a girl she didn't know from any of her classes, but she looked familiar. The lean blonde turned to look at her, and after eyeing Teagan's frame up and down, whispered, "Ah, the beginner dancers are supposed to be out there now."

"Thanks," Teagan answered tersely. "I'm well aware of that."

The girl scowled at her. "You don't exactly look like an experienced dancer." She turned her head toward the choreographer, clearly rolling her eyes in the process. Teagan was not impressed.

"Okay, let's listen up!" Liz belted out as she walked around the circle. When she reached Teagan her voice lowered as she said, "Ah, you have over five years of dance?" Inside Teagan was fuming. *"Great. Another anti-fat person."* She could almost hear the girl next to her snicker as she looked directly at the choreographer.

"Seven," she replied indignantly. She held the stare until Liz moved on and continued to the group.

"All of you in the second group should be watching the routine. I'll run through it with the first group a couple of times, and then I'll watch you do it alone. The second group will then get a chance to run the routine once before I add a couple of extra moves. After you've all danced I'll be calling a few of you out one last time." With that, dance auditions began, and Teagan watched intently as the first group danced. When they were finished, she joined the others in her group on the stage and found herself placed next to the blond girl.

"Great, I get the primadonna," Teagan thought. *"I guess it's time to show her that fat people can move just as well as she can."* The first routine was easy for her, and it felt wonderful to feel the music and move again.

She might need to head back to the dance studio where she and Joanne spent so many years together.

The second routine was more complicated, but nothing she couldn't handle. As she danced, she could see Beth in the front row. She moved just like her sister, and Teagan couldn't help but smile. *"Maybe better than her sister,"* she thought.

The director had returned from across the hall to watch the groups dance. Liz Patterson looked around and called seven girls, including Beth, the two girls from the dance studio that Teagan knew, and the snooty blond to the middle. She scanned the others, as if trying to decide who the eighth should be, when the director said, "The red head." Teagan watched as Liz did a double take toward her, and then faced the director defiantly. "Her?" she questioned, looking back. The director nodded, looking up at Teagan with curiosity. Teagan's eyes met his, and she stood taller and stepped into the last group.

When they finished, Teagan stood to catch her breath. The blond girl passed by, nonchalauntly saying, "Not bad – for a fat girl." Teagan's green eyes flashed in anger, and she thanked her sarcastically before heading over for music auditions. *"Just watch me,"* she thought, *"us fat girls can SING, too."*

A moment later, the two girls that Teagan knew from dance, Kyleigh and Julia, came up and hugged her. She was surprised to realize that she had really missed being at the studio, and was thrilled to have a couple of the girls closest to her back then be with her now.

"Teagan O'Sullivan, you made my day by getting back on stage!" Kyleigh said, her smile just lighting up her face. "You need to get your ass back down to the studio, girl! And soon!"

Julia was the quieter of the two. "We've missed you, girl. We know you needed a break – we all felt the loss, but know it was particularly hard on you. Miss Colleen always told us that you'd be back when you'd had time to heal a bit. She's gonna be so excited to hear that you're auditioning!"

"And that line you said to Patterson?" Kyleigh said with excitement. "*Seven.* My God, the look on her face was priceless -- especially when Mr. C. called you back for the final group. You go, girl, and show 'em all what you've got!"

Music auditions were much easier, with groups of eight starting off, and then individuals singing alone as the music director pointed. Some only sang a line before the next person was cued, and others sang several lines. Teagan was in a different group than the blond this time, standing off to the side with Beth next to her.

"I wish I knew who that blond was – I swear I've seen her before." Teagan whispered to Beth.

"Her?" Beth answered quietly. "All I know is that she's new this year. I think her name is Cassie."

As she spoke, Cassie began her solo lines, and Teagan immediately stopped to pay attention. "Damn, she can sing as well as she dances. Too bad her people skills suck."

Beth chuckled as they waited for their turn, and when called, they stood in front of the piano to begin. Out of the corner of her eye Teagan saw the girl Cassie leave her small group to go and stand next to a tall and attractive guy, Mike Blanchett, flashing him a big smile as she approached him. *"Figures, she's gotta be a flirt, too,"* she thought. As the opening bars of the audition song began, she immediately turned her focus to the song. It was the opening number of the show, and if she got the part of Hattie, she'd get to sing a solo. When the music director started the song the second time through, she began at the opposite end of the row, and the first couple of students only sang a line before she moved on. The next sang a couple, and then another was bypassed quickly until Beth was asked to sing.

Teagan stood beside her with both pride and some grief, as Beth's voice sounded just like her sister's before the anorexia took hold. She ended up singing three bars, and aside from a little nervousness she sounded wonderful. Teagan noticed that a lot of kids around the room had taken notice – probably because she was a freshman and did so well. She also noticed the director, Mr. Calabreschi, had entered quietly just in time to hear Beth sing. Finally Mrs. Kelly gave her the cue, and she opened her mouth to sing. She pictured herself at Caldwell Manor, singing for her favorite people, and had a blast as she gave it her all. The music director stood and watched her, letting her sing an entire four bars before signaling her to stop. As she moved on the last couple in the line, Beth reached over and squeezed Teagan's hand to congratulate her, and Teagan couldn't help but notice a few kids off to the side nodding their approval. Even Cassie had stopped flirting with Mike long enough to listen, standing there with her arms crossed against her chest and a scowl where her flashing smile had been. When the last group had finished, Liz Patterson addressed all of them. "If you should get a callback, then you'll also need to know the song 'Wunderbar' in case we want to hear you sing it. It might not be necessary, but please be prepared. Thanks for your cooperation – you all did a great job. Now you can head back over to the auditorium for final instructions."

Teagan and Beth walked back over to the auditorium together afterwards, and a few kids stopped to tell both of them how well they had sang on the way. Teagan felt satisfied for herself, and really excited for Beth. Across the hall they scanned the room for Brian, who was chatting with a guy she recognized from her English class, and they seemed to have hit it off.

When Brian spotted them, he waved, and turned to the guy to say goodbye. He approached and gave Beth a quick hug, saying, "Hey, kiddo, good to see you. It's been too long."

Beth returned the hug and grinned. "Thanks, you big lug. And happy birthday, by the way."

"You remembered?" Brian asked smiling. She nodded.

"I'll always remember your birthday because it was about month before Joanne's. Two fellow Scorpios – not easy to ignore. So how'd ya do?"

"Not too shabby," Brian replied, looking at Teagan as well. "And you guys?"

Beth spoke up first. "Teagan rocked both dance and voice. She'll get a callback for sure." Teagan smiled, and shared that Beth might as well.

"All right, kiddo – not an easy feat as a freshman. Your sis would be proud."

Beth's eyes watered a bit. "Thanks, guys. It was really good to have you both here."

As they all sat back down, Mr. C. got up to thank them all for coming. "Much as I'd love to cast all of you, the stage simple isn't that big. Callbacks will be this Wedneday, and you'll be notified by tomorrow. Cast list will be posted when you get back next week – and please know that just because you don't get a callback, it doesn't mean you didn't make the show. Be sure to check the cast list on the website, although I'll have Ann send out an email to everyone as well."

All were dismissed, and Beth waved goodbye as she headed out with a friend who was bringing her home. Teagan and Brian gathered their stuff and followed the others to the door.

"So," Brian began, "One promise kept – how do you feel?"

Teagan smiled with contentment. "Like I want a pizza to celebrate. Both auditions *and* your birthday. You game?"

Brian grinned. "I love it when a plan comes together."

CHAPTER 6

eagan woke up early the next morning, and immediately brought up her email only to find no word. *"Relax, girl, it's only 6:00 AM – I don't think stage managers get emails out quite that early."* She got herself ready for school and headed to the corner to meet Brian and a few other kids at the corner bus stop. Two stood off by themselves talking about a biology test, and the third stood with his earbuds blasting hip hop music loud enough to fend off conversation from anyone.

"Hope your mom wasn't mad that I grabbed you for your birthday dinner," Teagan said as she greeted him. She knew that Mrs. Morris hadn't made plans, but still felt a twinge of guilt.

"Nawh, she was fine. She ended up having to work an extra hour anyway, so she had a couple of slices of the leftovers I brought home. And she said to thank you for not making me sit home alone on my birthday." Teagan grinned, as Brian added, "Oh, and she stopped at the bake shop during her lunch hour to buy me a mocha cake for my dessert…..I tell ya, carrot cake for lunch and mocha cake for dinner? Best kind of birthday you can have!"

The bus approached and they got on, claiming two aisle seats a few rows back. Teagan recognized the girl in the seat beside her from auditions.

"Hi, you're Stephanie, right? I think I saw you at auditions yesterday."

The girl nodded and replied, "Yup, I was there. Hey, you're an amazing singer. How come you haven't been in shows until now?"

Teagan settled in, her butt hanging over the edge of the seat and almost touching Brian's leg. *They sure don't make bus seats for big people,* she thought. She smiled at Stephanie and replied. "I was in shows up until 7th grade at the middle school, but then took a few years off. How about you?"

Stephanie explained that she had moved to Caldwell in 8th grade. "I'm glad you came back to theater – a voice like yours should be on stage. Are you hoping to get the part of Kate?"

Teagan laughed. "I don't think that I'm cut out for that part – I'm going for Hattie, but would be totally happy in the ensemble. How about you?"

"Ensemble – always. I can sing and dance okay, and I have good facial expressions on stage – but my projection sucks. I'm fine with that. I'd hate to have to wear a microphone for the show and hear my voice coming through the sound system." She smiled genuinely as her phone started beeping, and in a moment she was enrapt in a text as Teagan turned back to Brian. They chatted about the upcoming day and promised to text each other if anyone heard anything about callbacks. When the bus arrived at school they went their separate ways for different classes, promising to meet back up at lunch time.

During her last class before lunch Teagan felt her phone vibrate, so she knew she had a text. "Callbacks up – will fill you in at lunch!" The last twenty minutes of Spanish seemed to drag, but soon enough she found Brian in a corner just inside the cafeteria. He was all excited and waved her over, his laptop already on and displaying the list. Teagan approached, knowing that his excitement meant that they had both gotten callbacks. She scanned down the list and found her name in alphabetical order.

TEAGAN O'SULLIVAN – CALLBACK FOR LILLI / KATE, HATTIE

She looked at the words, trying to process them as Brian let out a whoop. "I *knew* you'd be considered for the lead! You are gonna kick ass as Kate, girl!" Teagan looked again, not quite sure whether to believe it. "Brian, it's just a callback. I'm sure others are down as well – and I'd be thrilled to get Hattie. Wait – what about you?"

Brian beamed. "Call backs for both Hortensio and Paul. I'm excited about either. Oh, Teags, this is gonna be a great year!" Teagan sat down, both excited and in a little shock. She had never really pictured herself as someone that could pull off the role of Lilli. Her onstage character of Kate she was sure she could do, but the romantic lead? "How the hell am I qualified to try out for Lilli when I have no damn interest in anyone even holding my hand, never mind kissing me?" she asked.

Brian reached across and took her hand. "I already told ya, Teags – it's ACTING. Pretend it's Melvin at the nursing home."

Her belly shook as she laughed hard. "Now that's funny. I'll have to be sure to tell him what you said next time I work." Turning her attention back to his computer, she asked "So who else is on the list? And what does my competition look like?"

It didn't take long to see the name that jumped out at her:

CASSIE DURAND -- CALLBACK FOR LILLI / KATE, LOIS / BIANCA

"Oh, great, the snob that hates fat people is up against me – that might give me some motivation." She also found two other girls with callbacks for the main part, both of whom she knew. She looked for Beth's name, but didn't see it. Brian noticed her scrolling and surmised who she was looking for. "Hey, she's only a freshman – not surprising she's not there for a callback. I bet she still makes the ensemble."

Teagan nodded in agreement as she took out her lunch. She looked over at Brian who was still smiling and let out a deep sigh as the callback sank in. "So why am I all of a sudden really nervous?"

"Because," he said as reached over and grabbed a few of her grapes, "up until now you were just thinking about trying out and getting in to keep that promise to Joanne. But this isn't just about the promise anymore, Teags – this is something that you should do just for *yourself*. You're so damn talented, and it's about the time the rest of the world knew that as well."

That evening Teagan watched as many Youtube videos of the musical as she could find, just to see how other high schools and community theaters cast the role of Lilli / Kate. After she'd been listening to "Wunderbar" for about an hour, there was a knock on her bedroom door, and her mom popped her head in.

"Interested in a break? I just made a batch of popcorn."

Teagan nodded, and stood up and stretched. "I would *love* a break, mom – thanks." Peg O'Sullivan walked in with a big tray with two bowls of popcorn and two glasses of iced water as she joked, "Besides, if I had to listen to that song one more time I was going to go mad." Her eyes twinkled as she handed Teagan her bowl. "And you know I'm kidding, honey. How's it going?"

Teagan took a handful of popcorn and began munching, holding up a finger to signal to her mom that she had to wait a second. "God, that's good – thanks, mom." She took a swig of water, and then turned back to face her mom, who had sat down beside her on the bed. "Honestly, I don't know if I'm feeling more inadequate because of my weight or because I don't have a clue as to how to do romance – *or* any desire to learn. Any tips?"

"Honey, just be yourself. Just because you're aro doesn't mean that you can't express emotion. You love lots of people – maybe not romantically, but you still care about them. This couple in the show – they were together, and now they're apart, but still love each other. So think about Joanne – I know you guys weren't romantic, but I know how much you miss her and how excited you'd be to be together again – wouldn't that be 'wunderbar'?"

Teagan munched her popcorn thoughtfully. "Hadn't really thought about it that way, but yeah, I think I could use that for some motivation. Thanks, mom; you always give good advice."

Her mother leaned over and kissed her on the forehead and then stood up to go. "That's what mom's do. Now don't stay up too late tonight; you have a big day tomorrow."

Teagan agreed with a slight nod of her head. "Sure seems that way. Night, mom."

Callbacks were held the next afternoon right after school, and as Teagan and Brian entered the auditorium there was a sense of heightened excitement and nervousness. Ann the stage manager had them all sit in the first couple of rows, explaining that callbacks would be open, as the creative team wanted to be able to hear various students reading opposite each other. Some students would be asked to sing the song 'Wunderbar , although only a small portion of the song would be heard. She took attendance to be sure that everyone was present, and then turned it over to Mr. Calabreschi.

"Okay, folks, let's stay really focussed so I can get you out of here before the turkey comes out of the oven tomorrow," Mr. C. began. Everyone giggled and Teagan could feel the tension decrease just a little. "We'll start with the smaller roles and work our way to the leads. As soon as you've read for the parts you were called back for, you're free to leave – quietly. The last group will be just six or seven of you reading for Fred and Lilli. As I'm listening to one group, Ann will get the next group on deck. Everyone get it?" As all nodded, he clapped his hands once and smiled. "And don't forget that you guys are the cream of the crop – so show me what you've got and have fun! Cast list will go out next week -- now let's start, shall we?"

Teagan auditioned for the part of Hattie relatively early, and was told not to sing as she'd be sticking around for awhile. She watched three others also audition, with two being asked to sing. After that a lot of the smaller male roles were observed, and Teagan was thrilled to see Brian do so well with both of his roles.

Soon the group had narrowed down to about six girls and five boys, and auditions for the double cast roles of Bill/Lucentio and Lois/Bianca began. As she sat and waited, Teagan occasionally watched Cassie sitting next to Mike. He seemed relaxed and interested, and smiled a bit when Cassie laughed at something and let her hand rest on his arm for a moment. *so that's how flirting is done,* Teagan thought to herself. *"She definitely has an edge in THAT department, that's for sure."*

As Cassie was called up to read for the duel role of Lois/Bianca, she was asked to read opposite a guy Teagan recognized from Spanish, although she wasn't sure of his name. *"He must be another new kid in the past couple of years,"* she surmised, *"I know all the kids that have grown up in Caldwell."* She realized just how much she had detached from her peers in the past couple of years. Then again, they didn't have to deal with the grief that she'd had to work through.

Cassie was great on stage, and a natural at the role of Bianca as she flirted through her reading quite naturally. When she was asked to sing, her voice was gorgeous and almost perfect pitch. *"God, she can sing – AND act and dance,"* Teagan thought. *"If she wasn't such a nasty person she might even be someone I could be friends with."* She was curious to see how Cassie would do with the role of Lilli/Kate, but suspected that she would be her main competition.

When auditions got down to the last two roles, there were six left. Of the group, most had read for other roles as well, and Teagan felt that Mike Blanchett had the best shot at the main lead. Watching Cassie giggle and flash him a smile as they talked made her wonder if they wouldn't have the best chemistry together. Watching the two of them read together confirmed that they would be great together, and she began to doubt herself. *"Hattie will be a great role,"*, she thought.

But first it was her time to read for Lilli, and she ended up opposite Mike as well. She looked over the script and was at least glad that most of the audition was the bantering scene as Petruchio and Kate, and not the romance between Fred and Lilli. This she could at least handle. Sarcasm was one of her talents.

As they began their scene, she got lost in the role, forgetting about Cassie and the creative team, and really enjoying the barbs that she got to fling at Mike. His brown eyes flashed with amused intrigue, and he met her line after line as they brought the tension to life. When they got to the end of the scene, Teagan noticed Mr. C. watching her, sitting with the palms of his hands together in front of him, tapping his index fingers together as if he were deep in casting questions in his mind.

The music director had her sing, and she knew that she had nailed

"Wunderbar" before she was even half way through. When she finished, she sat back down to watch the last girl audition. She could feel Cassie's eyes on her, and when she turned to meet her gaze, she was met with a hostile glare. Teagan responded with a direct stare and a slight smile, throwing her own unspoken barb her way. All of sudden the idea of beating her out was a little exciting.

They were dismissed by 5:15, and while some left to find rides already waiting, there were a few that stood waiting in the hallway by the door until their rides showed up. Teagan found herself with Cassie and a girl named Paula, and prayed that Paula would be the one remaining with her. Unfortunately, Paula waved as her dad drove up, leaving the two contenders on opposite side of the hallway.

"You did a great job in there, Cassie," Teagan offered, trying to cut the tension. Cassie didn't respond, so she added, "I think you'll make a great Lilli."

Cassie's eyes flashed anger. "Well, if I don't, it won't be any thanks to you. Which I don't get, because normally the romantic lead isn't –" she cut herself off as she eyed Teagan's body up and down.

"Isn't fat?", Teagan replied. "Is that what you going to say?"

"You said it – not me," Cassie retorted with a smirk.

"Well, you know what? You're right. Most romantic leads are thin and beautiful and can fit into any dress in the costume department. But to assume that fat people can't act or sing or dance as well just because they're bigger is ridiculous."

Cassie glared at her. "But why would want to get out in *front* of people?"

Teagan could feel her anger rising. "You know what else? I happen to be comfortable with my fat. I *like* my curves. Damn it, I'm more comfortable in my size 20 body than you'll ever be in your size 8!"

As soon as she said the words, she regretted them. She could see the hurt in Cassie's face, followed by a cold stare. Cassie picked up her bag and stormed outside as she glared at Teagan and hissed "Whatever."

"Cassie, wait!" Teagan called as she opened the door. Cassie slowed but kept walking. "Look, that was out of line, and I'm sorry!" Cassie responded by climbing into her dad's car and slamming the door.

Teagan stood inside and ran her fingers through her hair. *"Way to go, Teagan. That was a disaster..."*

She hadn't noticed that Mike had exited the auditorium to catch the confrontation. When she saw him, she shook her head and sighed, wishing she could make all 220 pounds invisible.

"If it helps at all," Mike said, "I think she had that coming."

Teagan shook her head. "No, she didn't," she replied. "She hasn't been Miss Congeniality, but she didn't need to be blasted, either. Sometimes my people skills just suck."

Mike laughed. "Welcome to the human race. Hey, you apologized, and that counts for something. She can be pretty damn judgmental, and it was kind of nice to hear someone put her in her place. I think you might have a whole lot of Kate in you, just sayin'."

Teagan caught sight of her mom driving up. She smiled at Mike and thanked him for the support. "I guess time will tell," she said. "Hey, have a Happy Thanksgiving – and enjoy your turkey."

"You, too."

"Oh, don't worry," Teagan said with a smirk, "I *always* enjoy my turkey.....and stuffing, and potatoes, and pies as well." With that, she grabbed her bag, smiled at Mike, and strolled out the door, leaving him to watch her curves with intrigue.

CHAPTER 7

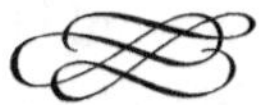

Teagan's first thoughts the next morning were about the callbacks, and as she considered whether she might actually be cast as Lilli she felt the butterflies in her stomach start to flutter. As she often did when she needed to talk, she lay in bed and spoke out loud to Joanne.

"Okay, Joanne, I did it," she began, looking at the various photos of the two of them still next to her bed, "and now I've got the weekend to wait to find out if I end up with the part that you should have had." She knew Joanne would have been the perfect choice for Lilli, and she thought of how wonderful it would have been to have played Hattie alongside her best friend. "It would have been 'wunderbar'," she said sadly.

She looked at a couple of photos from her 7th grade play at Caldwell Middle School, where she and Joanne had played sisters and Brian had been their neighbor. The "three musketeers", their parents called them that year. The three of them really had grown up together, and Teagan would forever remember that show as being one of the highlights of their time together. Little did she know it would be the last time they got to share the stage together. By the time 8th grade rolled around, Joanne's anorexia had become too powerful to overcome, despite her constant claims that she had everything under control. She was hospitalized the day after Halloween and died two weeks later as her heart and kidneys gave out.

Teagan and Brian spent all of 8th grade in therapy and grief support, and slowly learned to live life without their best friend. "Thank God Brian was still here," she told Joanne in the photo, "or I don't know how either one of us would have pulled through."

Teagan decided she'd wallowed long enough, and got up and dressed to help her mom with Thanksgiving preparations before heading off to work. The residents would be having their annual Thanksgiving dinner at 1:00 today, and she had volunteered to work and do some activities with residents who were alone or those who had family visiting. It was always a fun day. That night she'd head home in time for a turkey dinner with her parents and her mother's sister, who lived several towns away.

She found her mom in the kitchen cutting up squash, and already the smells of an apple pie in the oven were starting to permeate the room.

"Hmm, it smells heavenly in here," Teagan said as she greeted her with a hug. "Good morning – and thanks for letting me sleep in. I'll help with the potatoes if you want."

Peg O'Sullivan returned the hug and replied, "Just sit and have breakfast and keep me company. I know you have to work today."

Teagan smiled and poured herself a cup of coffee, and grabbed a bagel to prepare for breakfast. "Where's Dad this morning?" she asked as she placed the bagel in the toaster and then opened the refrigerator for cream cheese.

"He should be back shortly, " her mom said. "He just went out for a short walk this morning. Said he wanted to burn off a few calories before replenishing them three fold later."

Teagan laughed as she sat down. "Can hardly wait for that turkey later on. What time is Aunt Mary coming over?"

"She said she'd be here by 4:00, and I figured we'd have dinner on the table waiting for you when Dad picks you up at 5:00. So no extra chatting today at the end of your shift!" Her green eyes twinkled as she shook the knife in Teagan's direction.

"Got it," Teagan mumbled as she took a bite of her bagel, and as she chewed she heard her dad returning from his walk.

"God, it smells good in here!" he reported as he entered. "Can hardly wait to add the smell of that bird later on. Hey, morning, sweetie – how'd the audition go?" He gave his wife a hug and refilled his coffee cup, and then sat down next to Teagan to hear her summary of the callbacks.

"So now we just wait until Monday to see what happens," Teagan finished.

Teagan's dad reached over to pat her hand. "I'm really proud of you, honey. I know it wasn't easy, but I think you'll be glad to get back to into theater for these last two years of high school. It'll be good for you."

Peg O'Sullivan nodded in agreement. "And I know it's what Joanne would have wanted, even if she won't be there with you."

Teagan took a sip of coffee and then shared, "But there might be another Newton on stage. Beth tried out, and she looked great in auditions. I sure hope she makes the ensemble."

"Wow. Little Beth is in high school already?" her dad asked. "Time really is flying by, isn't it?"

"Speaking of which," Peg noted as she turned to Teagan, "you mentioned helping with potatoes, and if your offer still stands I'll take you up on it." She took an apron off of a hook by the refrigerator and threw it at her daughter. "Because we simply can't have Thanksgiving dinner without potatoes. It's just not done." Teagan chuckled, tying the extra long ties around her big hips and grabbing a cutting board.

Teagan's dad dropped her off at Caldwell Manor at 12:45, and she could tell from the extra cars in the lot that there were lots of visitors, which made her happy. The residents loved having their families come to see them, even if only for holidays and special events. Those with family that came on a regular basis were the minority, and often envied by their peers. Then there were those who had little or no family, and the staff became their "family" – especially on holidays.

Teagan always volunteered to work on holidays, as she loved using music to help lift the spirits of those that might be spending the holiday alone.

Melvin greeted her first as she entered, as he often sat near the main lobby and greeted all visitors as they came in. "Miss Teagan!! Happy Thanksgiving! It's almost time for turkey!"

She laughed as she hung up her coat. "That's what I like – a man with his priorities straight! Happy Thanksgiving, Melvin! Did you help to cook it?"

"Nawh, the women in the kitchen did the cooking. I watched the parade. It was a windy day and I thought the balloons were gonna take off and fly."

Teagan chuckled as they walked together toward the dining room. The staff had decorated beautifully and added extra tables for visiting family members, and many were seating themselves in preparation for the meal. Teagan spotted Ida who was just being wheeled up to a table by an attractive woman with the same dark complexion, and she knew it had to be her daughter Eliana. Beside her was a tall man, and a young teen boy lagged behind. *That must be Philip,* Teagan thought. She looked for the missing family member – Cassandra – but didn't see her.

Teagan got Melvin settled and then went over to greet the Vassilikas family. Ida's eyes lit up when she saw Teagan approaching, and she reached out and warmly grasped her hand. "Teagan! I want you to meet my family. This is my daughter Eliana, her husband Frank, and their son, Philip."

Teagan shook hands with each of them. "I've heard so much about you," she said, "and it's a pleasure to finally meet you. But where is Cassandra? I was hoping to finally meet her."

Eliana looked surprised that Teagan knew her by name. "Sadly, she wasn't feeling well this morning, and didn't want to risk getting her grandmother sick."

Teagan put her hand on Ida's shoulder. "That's too bad, although it was sweet of her to forego Thanksgiving dinner for the sake of this beautiful lady." Ida reached up and squeezed her hand as she looked up at Teagan and smiled.

Philip scowled. "She just didn't wanna come, that's all."

Eliana turned to her son and reprimanded him. "Now, Philip, that's just not true. Nobody would pass up a Thanksgiving dinner to stay home alone unless they were sick."

"Someday," Ida said to Teagan, "you're finally going to meet that granddaughter of mine. I still think the two of you would hit it off."

"Well, I look forward to it, because any granddaughter of yours has to be wonderful," Teagan said as she excused herself to go and help serve dinner. "Enjoy your visit, and I'll catch up with you later on." She gave Ida a quick wink and headed to the back of the dining room where staff were gathering to grab serving platters of food. Today she'd get *two* Thanksgiving dinners – here, and later at home. It was a day to be grateful, for sure.

Once the residents had all eaten, staff were allowed to fill their plates and sit together for a meal. Teagan eagerly grabbed a plate and got in line next to one of the young nurses. As she heaped her plate with turkey and stuffing, the nurse raised her eyebrows. "Aren't you eating dinner with your folks later?" she asked.

Teagan nodded with a twinkle in her eye. "This is my appetizer."

The nurse shook her head. "Honey, you should lay off the carbs a little and have more salad. That way you can enjoy your full meal later without feeling guilty."

Teagan laughed as she reached for the gravy. "Sue, I know you mean well, but I have NO intention of cutting carbs from either meal. This is a holiday, and I'm gonna enjoy it, just like I'll enjoy the leftovers tomorrow."

Sue smiled weakly, but the disapproval was there. "Well, maybe after the holidays, then. You know, with all the New Year's resolution people. After all, you have such a pretty face." Teagan groaned inside as they headed to separate tables to eat. She'd love a dollar for every time she heard about her "pretty face", and the implication that she should have an attractive, thin body to match.

After dinner Teagan had faciliated a group reminiscing hour, where residents and family members shared memories about Thanksgivings over the years. By the time most family members had left, Teagan had a Lawrence Welk holiday special all ready for residents to watch. She knew many would fall asleep at this point, so she had some simple board games set up for those that were more alert, and the rest enjoyed the music that welcomed the upcoming holiday season. Teagan knew they'd be singing Christmas carols from now on every time she worked, and that made her smile.

She found Ida sitting quietly at a table doing a crossword puzzle, and she grabbed a chair and sat down to join her for a few minutes. "How was your visit with your family?"

Ida put her pen down and smiled. "It was lovely, my dear. At first Eliana had proposed having me to the house for the day to eat there, but I honestly didn't know if I wanted to go back. I think I've transitioned rather well to living here, and I didn't want a bunch of memories to make me doubt my choices. Does that make sense?"

Teagan nodded. "You amaze me. I've known so many residents that come here feeling angry and depressed that they are losing their homes and all their possessions, and that their families don't care. And here you are, feeling grateful and content for a new chapter of your life. We should get you on the marketing brochures."

Ida chuckled and posed, as if for the camera. "Why not? I wish more could embrace the change of being here. The staff are wonderful, the food is good, and the activities keep our minds and bodies working. How is that not better than sitting home staring at four walls? I feel bad for those that spend their final years alone and depressed. Life's too short to sit around being lonely."

"Were you ever lonely?" Teagan inquired.

"Absolutely, my dear – everybody is some of the time. Especially in my younger years, and even during my marriage there were lonely times. Sometimes I think I got happier the older I got and the more independence that I had. And I could choose the people that I wanted in my life."

Teagan listened wistfully. "I can relate to that…..and how hard it is to lose them along the way."

Ida looked pensively at her. "I can tell that I've struck a chord – there's a sadness in your eyes just now that tells me you've lost someone special."

Teagan teared up and nodded slightly. "Her name was Joanne. She and I grew up together here in Caldwell, and were like sisters. She passed away three years ago when we were starting 8th grade."

Ida grasped her hands and squeezed them. "Oh, my dear, that must have been so hard. Can I ask what happened?"

Teagan wiped a tear from her eyes, as remembering always brought back the longing. "She died because of complications from her eating disorder. She had anorexia, and just refused to believe it was that bad until it was too late. I tried so hard to reach her, but she just lashed out as time went on. But I never dreamed that she'd actually die."

Ida patted her hand gently. "I can only imagine how much that must have hurt."

Teagan nodded through misty eyes. "For months I didn't wanna get out of bed and go to school, and I quit all the theater and dance stuff I'd done all my life. It was a rough year. And one of the loneliest times of my life."

"I'm so sorry, honey – I had no idea." She reached up to stroke the girl's hair, and gave her an understanding smile. "But look at you now. It's clear that you've worked hard to get back to where you are today, and that shows such inner strength."

"My friend Brian helped a lot there," Teagan acknowledged. "He was the third musketeer of the group and took it hard as well, but he was determined that it wouldn't turn us both into bitter and depressed teens. God, I can't imagine life without him these past few years."

Ida's eyes twinkled. "Ahh, is this Brian special then?"

Teagan laughed. "If you mean romantically, than no. He's like a brother to me, but I've never felt anything even slightly romantic toward him. Besides, I don't think I'm quite his type, if you get the idea."

Ida smiled knowingly and nodded. "Well, someday I'd like to meet this young man anyway. He's special to me because he helped you through a hard time, and you're special to me because…" She paused for a moment as she found the words, "…because you remind me of my Cassandra. Maybe not the current version, but definitely her growing up. That's another meeting that still has to happen someday. And soon, I hope."

Teagan patted her hand and pushed her chair back, as a glance at the clock told her it was time to put things away before her dad arrived to pick her up.

"I look forward to that, Ida," she said. "And if she's anything like you then I know I'll like her – quite a lot. But alas, it's time that I get ready to go. I'll have to fill you in on everything else that's been going on in my life next time. Good night. I'm so grateful that you moved here."

CHAPTER 8

The weekend dragged by. After a busy holiday Teagan tried to pass the time with studying, making a Christmas gift list, and watching "Kiss Me Kate" multiple times. That Sunday her dad talked her into taking a break and going out for breakfast, and they hit the Caldwell Diner just before the church crowd arrived.

The hostess greeted them warmly. "Booth or table?" Teagan's dad chose the latter, for which she was grateful. Sometimes squeezing into a booth was uncomfortable. She hated having the edge of the table pushing against her gut as she was trying to enjoy a meal. She arranged her chair a bit farther out from the table to allow some space, and then nodded along with her dad when the waitress came asked about coffee.

"Whatcha havin'?" her dad asked.

"I know it won't be anything turkey related." They both chuckled, as the post-holiday leftovers were waning and most were looking forward to other food again. Teagan checked over the menu, and made her choice as the waitress returned with coffee.

"I'll have a western omelet, sausage links, home fries with onion, and rye toast."

Her dad folded his menu, winked at the waitress, and said, "I'll have the same – we'll make it easy for ya." He sipped his coffee and looked around the diner. "You can tell church hasn't gotten out yet – we just beat 'em all."

Teagan looked out the window to the church across the street, and its full parking lot confirmed the observation. She glanced at the clock, and replied, "It's just about 10:00 – so brace yourself."

Their food arrived just as the church service was letting out, and as predicted, a line soon formed at the door. Caldwell Diner was always busy, but never more so than Sunday mornings when the church services were over.

As Teagan cut into her sausage she saw one of the kids that had tried out for show heading past with her family. She was surprised when the girl stopped at her table.

"Morning! Are you going crazy like I am? I mean, why Mr. C. couldn't have posted the list BEFORE the weekend I'll never know, but this day is going to last forever." She looked at Teagan's dad and her voice dropped. "Hey."

"Dad, this is Paula Williams. Paula, no big mystery – this is my dad."

He smiled as he swallowed his sausage. "Nice to meet you, Paula – although you look a little familiar."

Teagan nodded. "Paula was in shows with me years ago. We just never really connected back then." Turning back to Paula, she added "And yes, this day is gonna be *long!*"

"I'm just glad I wasn't up for Lilli 'cause you rocked that audition! Gotta run – and good luck!"

Teagan sipped her coffee as she noticed her dad watching Paula's departure, slightly nodding his head.

"What was *that* for?" she asked, referring to the nod.

"Just that I think this is going to be a good year for you – that's all." He took a bite of his toast. "It'll be nice for you to get reacquainted with some of the theater and dance kids from middle school. And maybe make some new friends, too."

Teagan listened as she spread jelly on her toast. "I suppose --

although a lot of the kids from back then have formed their own little social circles over the years. I'm not sure I'll fit in that easily."

Her dad finished his coffee, and signaled to the waitress for a refill. "Just give it a chance, honey. I'm sure a lot of them remember Joanne, too – and some of them might be missing her as well." He took a bite of his bacon, and added, "okay, end of lecture."

Teagan smiled at him, and added more ketchup to her potatoes. It was definitely something to think about, but for now, she was going to enjoy the rest of her breakfast.

The next day dragged on even longer than the one when callbacks had been posted. The cast list would be posted right at the end of the day – probably so the director could book out of school and not face the disappointments and celebrations first hand. Teagan remembered what that was like from middle school, when you faced your competition for the first time after one had gotten super excited while the other felt the rejection. *"Theater is not for the thin-skinned, that's for sure."*

She met Brian at the end of the day and headed to the bulletin board outside the auditorium, where luckily noone else was congregated at the moment. As they got closer, Teagan stopped.

"Go look for me, Brian," she said, "I don't think I can."

She watched him take the last few steps and peruse the list, and then tried to read his face as he turned to face her.

"Well?" she asked hesitantly.

Brian nearly jumped into the air as he came toward her in a leap as his arms wrapped around her.

"You got *Lilli!* I *knew* you were gonna – I just *knew!*"

Teagan stood frozen, not quite believing his words. She then needed to see her name in print, proving it was true, so she took a few steps forward to see the list. As Brian had reported, there it was, right at the top of the list. She'd gotten the lead.

Her hands came up over her mouth as she whispered "oh, my God," still in shock. "I was sure that Cassie –"

Brian finished her sentence. "She got Bianca, and she'll be perfect for it. Teags, you *did* it! And I'm so damn proud of you!"

Teagan stood there for a moment letting it all sink in. Not only had she kept her promise, but she'd nailed the female lead – the part she was sure Joanne would have had. And now she finally allowed herself to feel the excitement of what she'd just accomplished.

"I still can't believe it," she said, her hands actually shaking a bit. She leaned against the wall for a second, and then realized that she was curious about the rest of the cast. Especially about who would be playing opposite her. She turned back to the list and wasn't at all surprised to see Mike Blanchett's name. She also realized she wanted to find Brian's name.

"Where are you?" she asked excitedly.

Brian pointed to his name. "I got Paul – and I'm really psyched for that, 'cause I get to sing and dance in 'Too Darn Hot.' And Teags, look," he said as his finger moved down the list, "Beth not only made the ensemble, but she's a featured dancer as well."

Teagan's eyes filled up seeing the last name "Newton" on the list, wishing it could have been the older sister, but thrilled that Beth would be on the stage with her.

"You know, I think God knew I wouldn't be ready until Beth was here to join us. I can't tell you how excited I am to have her share this with us."

Brian nodded as they heard noises behind them. Several kids were heading down to check the list, and Brian grabbed her arm and pulled her toward the door.

"Come on, Teags, " he said with some urgency, "Let's get out of here before the crowd shows up. I wanna take you to Gino's to celebrate with just us!"

Teagan didn't need any additional encouragement, and zipped out the door ahead of him.

CHAPTER 9

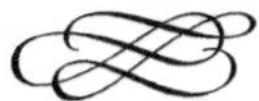

The first rehearsal of the show took place the Monday before the Christmas break began. It was called a "read through", where scripts were handed out and the cast was introduced to each other. They then sat together on stage and read through the script for the first time with each person reading their part. Teagan sat through her last class feeling the butterflies in her stomach again. While excited about being on stage again, she was nervous about the major role she had been assigned.

"Jeez, Teagan," she thought to herself as she doodled in her notebook, *"get over it. You've done lots of shows in the past, and you did fine. You don't get that rusty after just a few years."* She knew it wasn't her acting ability as much as being in the spotlight.

While she was comfortable in her own skin, she also knew there was prejudice against fat people. She'd faced it during auditions with the choreographer, and especially with Cassie. She wondered if they'd accept her now or if more confrontations lay ahead. She didn't really want to spend the time defending herself for who she was.

Besides her size, she also knew at some point she'd have to be more open about being asexual and aromantic, and she wasn't sure how much of a stigma she'd be facing. She remembered her mom's words the night before auditions: "Just be yourself." She smiled and sighed, doodling the words into her notebook as a reminder. As the final bell rang, she closed her notebook, grabbed her purse, and headed off to put the advice into practice.

Beth greeted her at the door of the auditorium with a big hug, saying "I am SO excited for you! You're gonna be wonderful!"

Teagan gave her a squeeze as she heard a familiar voice behind her.

"She's gonna rock it, ain't she?" Brian joined the group hug, and then Beth stepped back and looked more serious.

"Joanne would be SO proud of you. And you know she's gonna be your very own guardian angel through this whole production."

Teagan nodded wistfully. "She'll watch over ALL of us," she said. "And I am SO glad that you're here to step into the third musketeer's shoes, Beth. Your sister is equally proud of YOU."

"By the way, are you guys free Saturday night? My mom was hoping you could both come for dinner. You know, for Joanne's birthday—and yours, too, Brian."

"Wouldn't miss it, kid."

Teagan nodded along with him. "No place else we'd rather be. But for right now", she continued, "I think we'd better get to it, huh?"

When they reached the stage Teagan noticed that Beth nodded to them and headed off to sit with a few other freshmen who had made the show. She and Brian were able to get seats together, and on her other side sat Paula, who had been assigned the role of Hattie.

"Hey, Paula, congrats on being Hattie. I remember your audition was phenomenal. And you had one of the leads in 8th grade, didn't you?"

Paula nodded. "Yeah, but this is my first major role in high school. Congrats, yourself. I was really happy to see you come back. I'm sure the last few years have been tough, after…" she hesitated nervously, not sure if it was a topic to bring up.

"It's okay, Paula, you can say it," Teagan replied knowingly. "And you're right, losing Joanne was the toughest thing I've ever gone through. But after some time to work through it, I'm glad to be back.

Some of my happiest memories are from theater. And thanks for caring. I wasn't sure how many really knew what happened."

Paula looked at her pensively. "I think everyone *knew* what happened, but hardly anyone talked about it. The teachers at school gave a short explanation the day after she died, and some kids from theater talked to counselors a few times, but none of us knew Joanne like you and Brian did."

Teagan was about to respond when Anne Richards clapped her hands loudly to get attention. "We'll talk more later," she whispered.

The conversations quickly became murmurs and then stopped as all eyes turned toward Anne. She was standing with a clip board and a pencil next to a small table where Mr. Calabreschi, Liz Patterson, and Mrs. Kelly sat. On the table in front of Mrs. Kelly was a portable stereo system, and Teagan surmised that they'd be hearing some of the music as well.

"Okay, gang, let's get started!," Ann began. "I'll be taking attendance really quickly and introducing the cast as I go. As your name is called, please come up to the table to get your scripts. Ensemble members can take any of the scripts in the blue box, but be sure that you write down your script number on the sheet in front of Mr. C. Those with speaking parts will have a script with your name on it already, and they'll be handed to you by Mrs. Kelly and Ms. Patterson. When I call off your name, acknowledge your presence any way you see fit. And remember to PROJECT!"

The cast laughed as attendance got underway. As names were called, Teagan knew most of the cast, but there were quite a few peers that had moved to Caldwell in the past few years. While her neighborhood in town hadn't changed a lot over time, she knew there were several new developments at either end of town that had been built more recently. Most of them had huge houses, and a lot of the old timers did nothing but complain about the new "fancy folk" building their mansions on the old farmland, and then heading into Boston on the train every day so that they could afford to spend a litle time in their fancy houses on the weekend.

As the speaking parts were announced, the cast clapped for each actor, and she cheered extra loud for Brian as he got up to get his script. When Cassie was called up as Lois/Bianca Teagan clapped along with everyone else. She hoped she'd be able to apologize further for her outburst after auditions. Cassie sat back down next to Mike and pulled her coat over her shoulders, adding to the layered shirt and sweatshit that she already wore.

As Teagan was announced, she felt her face flush a bit as she walked up to accept her script. Mike Blanchett was right behind her to finish out the cast introductions, and then Mr. C. got up to address the cast.

"So now that we all know each other, we're gonna get to know the show. For those of you that might not be familiar with it, 'Kiss Me, Kate' is about a theater group putting on a show – in this case, they are performing a production of Shakespeare's 'Taming of the Shrew', which explains why most of you have two roles or two ensembles listed next to your names. Almost everyone who is in the ensemble will be portraying both the actors in Baltimore, as well as villagers in Italy."

He smirked a bit as he continued, "And that means that ALL of you will be 'Brushing Up Your Shakespeare' for this production." Some of the cast groaned from his pun on one of the song titles, while others were thinking of having to speak in Shakespeare's manner. As if he read their minds, he added, "Look, I know a lot of you are NOT well versed in iambic pentameter, which is the rythym, or meter, that Shakespeare is written in. I also know that some of the languge will be unfamilar to you – especially today as we're just beginning. So do the best you can and we'll stop and explain each scene as we go so that you'll be able to understand the storyline at least."

"Finally," he continued, "We'll do the first act, and then we'll take a half hour dinner break over in the music room with pizza and salad before coming back to act two. We should be done by 8:00 tonight, and then tomorrow you'll have music with Mrs. Kelly, and Thursday you'll have choreography with Ms. Patterson. That'll be it until after break, and you better all come back with a good handle on your lines. January and February will fly by faster than you can imagine."

He looked around at the group. If you have any questions, write them down and talk to me at dinner." With that, he grabbed his binder, opened it, and turned to Paula. "Okay, Hattie, take us away!"

As the read through progressed, Teagan got lost in her character, and found herself already giving both the roles of Lilli and Kate unique voices. She found that most of the leads did the same, and she was impressed with some of her cast mates and their talent. It was clear that Mr. C. knew how to cast a show, even if occasionally she wondered why he had chosen her. It became clearer when she began reading her lines as Kate, as she just loved Shakepeare's language, and especially the barbs that flew out of her mouth to those she interacted with. She found many of her peers watching her intently, and she grew more confident as the first act went on in her ability to carry it off.

Her one scene with Cassie, where Kate and her sister Bianca are fighting, went particularly well. Cassie seemed more animated than in any other scene, and Teagan suspected some of the anger was coming from within the actress. Regardless of the motivation, Teagan matched her tone as the vocal sparring flowed between them. *"Well, if nothing else,"* Teagan thought, *"we'll have some great chemistry for hating each other."*

Her read through of the Fred and Lilli scenes were a little awkward. She did fine on the sarcastic scenes, but felt more inadequate when their dialogue got reminiscent of old memories in love. She could feel Brian nudge her with his elbow every now and then, and she could almost hear him whispering, "It's ACTING, Teags....."

By the time dinner break rolled around, Teagan was feeling both exhilarated and hungry. She was surprised when several of the cast came over to tell her how great she sounded, and more so that a couple welcomed her back after being away for a few years. She lost track of Brian, who had gone to grab a box of cookies that he made for dessert, but walked across the hall with Paula and a few other kids she'd known since middle school.

"Maybe it won't be so bad getting to know some of these kids again," she thought. *"So far, at least, things are pretty good."*

Brian caught up with her in line, and Teagan found herself moving along the food table on the opposite side from Cassie and Mike. As Teagan filled her salad bowl to the brim and grabbed two slices of pizza, she noticed Cassie's half a bowl of salad and one slice. It was just another reminder of the girl that should have been there across the table – but wasn't.

She sat with Brian, Paula, and several others, but her attention was drawn repeatedly to watching Cassie at the next table. She talked a lot to Mike and the two girls with them, playing with her salad as she occasionally took a small bite. Teagan noticed she hadn't touched her pizza yet.

When Brian walked around passing out his cookies, she watched Mike take a handful while Cassie shook her head. She could hear her response despite the distance between them. "No chocolate for me. I'm too fat for those!" Mike turned to say something like "Yeah, right," as he munched on his cookies. He must have said something about her pizza as well, because Teagan watched Cassie slide her plate toward him, gesturing that she was full or too excited to eat. Mike didn't hesitate to pick up the slice and finish off his meal with a little more pizza.

When Brian got to her with cookies, she automatically grabbed three and took a bite. Immediately she turned to her friend with a smile, "These are delicious, Brian. Coconut again?" Brian nodded.

"German Chocolate Cake Cookies, for our unit on Germany this week. I made an extra batch over the weekend to bring tonight."

Paula licked her lips with approval, and one of the other guys at the table turned to Brian and spoke on behalf of everyone eating. "Dude, you can bring these ANY time. They're awesome!" As Teagan chewed on her last cookie, she glanced over as Cassie got up to throw her plates away, and noticed even a little salad still in the bowl. Once again the butterflies in her stomach signaled her stress levels rising, but this time it was for an all too familiar feeling that Cassie might have a lot more in common with her former best friend than she thought. As they all headed back over to the auditorium she hoped that she was wrong.

CHAPTER 10

A few days passed and Teagan said goodbye to Brian as the bus stopped by Caldwell Manor after school. She was tired from the past two days of rehearsals, but excited to be back to work with the residents, who seemed to be the most accepting people she'd ever known. She was particularly looking forward to talking to Ida and telling her all about the show. She realized that Ida had quickly become her favorite resident, and extra special to her.

Karen Drake was coming out of the main office and greeted her. "That's what I like to see. My employees smiling as they walk in the door."

Teagan laughed as she said hello. "Hey, you know how much I love working here!"

Karen nodded. "You're the best activity aide I've ever had – I hope you know that. And I got your message about the flexible hours after Christmas. You give me your rehearsal schedule, and I promise I'll work all of your hours around it. And congratulations on getting such a great role! We'll have to plan a resident field trip to come and see you."

Teagan beamed. "That would be the best audience in the whole world," she said. Changing the subject, she asked, "By the way, is

Charlotte around? I have a question I need to ask her, and was wondering if I could clock in ten minutes late if she's able to chat."

"She just left the meeting ahead of me, so you should be able to catch her in her office. And clock in for your normal time. You've more than made up for it over the years." With that, Karen headed off down the hall to the activity room, and Teagan went around the corner to see if the nurse was indeed in her office.

Charlotte looked up as Teagan poked her head in the door.

"Teagan, how are you? And hey, I heard at the meeting that we have a new star in our facility. Congratulations!"

"Thanks. It's still kind of a shock at times, but I'm pretty excited about it most of the time. Do you have a couple of minutes?"

Charlotte closed the folder she'd been writing in and gestured for Teagan to sit down.

"My door is always open – unless it's change of shift or we're short. What's on your mind, Teagan?"

Teagan sat and took a second to collect her thoughts, and then took a deep breath.

"I'm not sure if this is even an issue, or maybe I'm just super sensitive about it, but I've noticed a girl at rehearsal that's setting off some red flags in my head."

Charlotte looked perplexed as she said, "I'm not quite following you."

"It goes back to Joanne," she started, watching the serious look appear on Charlotte's face. "It may be nothing, but I've noticed some little behaviors that Joanne used to have, and I'm just not sure what's normal behavior and what's – "

"An eating disorder?" Charlotte finished for her. Teagan nodded, tears welling up as she blinked them away. She was still surprised at times when the emotions overcame her, but sitting here with a nurse who clearly understood the issues just brought the urgency to the surface.

"I might be totally out of line, because I'm not in tune with girls today and their whole fixation on diets and being thin, but something about her just jumped out at me. Or maybe since I'm writing a paper on anorexia I'm just looking for things that aren't even there."

"Tell me some of the things you've seen."

Teagan shared the events of the pizza dinner, and then started to feel foolish.

"It's probably nothing at all. Being a fat girl who has never gotten into the whole diet scene makes me a freak in some ways. I just don't get how society can be so damn judgemental over a person's size. And now I feel like I'm totally overacting with this one event," she admitted. "She was probably just trying to impress the guy she was sitting with."

"That's possible," Charlotte reponded, "but don't just write it off. If your inner gut was sending off signals, then trust those. If this girl DOES have a problem, then it's imperative that she get help for it as early as possible. All the studies show that the earlier anorexia is treated the better the chances for – "

Charlotte stopped mid-sentence, aware of the impact of her statement.

Teagan ended the line for her, "For survival? It's okay, Charlotte. I've worked through a lot of crap after Joanne died. The first year I felt guilty, thinking I should have recognized the early signs. But I *knew* Joanne. I don't know this girl at all. I don't even *like her.* But God forbid, if it IS the beginning, then I'd do anything to keep it from taking another –" She stopped short, as she realized that she was about to say "friend", and Cassie was surely anything but.

Charlotte didn't seem to mind that she'd left the sentence unfinished. "Just stay aware," she suggested, "and talk to the other kids as well; see if others are seeing the same things. Now tell me about this paper you're writing."

Teagan filled her in on her assignments, and Charlotte listened intently.

"Teagan, that's commendable – I know it won't be easy for you, but the world needs to be educated, and you can help with that. I'd love to read it when you're done with it."

Teagan nodded as she got up to head down the hall. "Thanks for your time," she said. "I just needed to know that I wasn't crazy."

Charlotte got up and gave her a hug. "And listen, if it DOES start to look like Joanne all over again, you need to let someone know. If *you* can't talk to her, then someone else should, got it?"

Teagan nodded, hoping that would never be the case. The prospect of having to talk to Cassie about something so serious was something she couldn't even imagine.

As she headed into the activity room she was met by Melvin, Kitty, and Gladys at the door. They had heard the news about her audition results and presented her with a big congratulations card with stickers and glitter. She was thrilled by their enthusiasm, and even more so when they started telling every resident that joined them for their music session.

Teagan was happy to see Ida wheeling herself into the room, and they locked eyes and greeted each other with a smile. Kitty was dancing in the middle of the room and singing "Wunderbar" at the top of her lungs. A couple of residents were trying to get her to be quiet, saying that it wasn't a Christmas song. Kitty then told them that it was a song that Teagan would be singing in her lead role as Lilli. All eyes then turned toward her confirmation.

"Yes, guys, what they are saying is true; I'm going playing the role of Lilli in the musical 'Kiss Me, Kate' at the high school later this year. 'Wunderbar' is one of the songs that I'll be performing, although not nearly as well as Kitty just did for you."

They all laughed as Kitty took a bow and sat down.

Gladys raised her hand as if still in school. "So what's your favorite song to sing in the whole thing?"

Teagan didn't hesitate a bit. "Well, I haven't actually started working on it yet, but I know my favorite will be a song called 'I Hate Men.'" The women all clapped as Melvin scowled in a good mannered way. Ida just sat and let her face express her approval. Teagan loved how the wrinkles around her eyes just brought her face to life when she was happy.

She decided it was time to redirect them all back to the present, and once she started in on the first Christmas carol all minds followed. Alternating between religious carols and more popular tunes worked well to keep everyone happy, and before long it was time to end the singing so that residents could have a little time before dinner.

Teagan was putting things away as residents all filed out of the room, but Ida stayed behind and smiled.

"I've missed you, my dear. I know it's only been a few days, but I have to admit that I look forward to the days when you are scheduled to work more than any others.."

Teagan closed the cabinet and grabbed a cleaning rag to wipe down the tables, speaking as she worked. "I'm glad to hear that Ida, because I was thinking earlier today how quickly you've taken over as the number one resident in my book."

She watched Ida's eyes twinkle once again, and went to sit next to her when she finished the last table.

"So how are you?" she asked her. "Anything new and exciting happen the past couple of days?"

Ida chuckled. "No – and that's a good thing. I enjoy having a quiet and boring life at long last. Let's see….I've finished the book I was reading about Italy, had a lovely visit from Eliana this morning, got through another book of crossword puzzles, and am now halfway through a lame murder mystery where I picked out the killer on page 42. How's that for exciting?"

Teagan laughed out loud. "You sound as exciting as I am most of the time," she answered. "I'm wondering how long it will be before I'm envious of your quiet schedule. I look at my calendar now and wince. Between work and rehearsals, I feel that my life has just disappeared and will remain missing for the next several months."

Ida smiled. "So, tell me all about this new role of yours. I'm not as familiar with this show as a lot of other musicals, but I think it's based on a Shakespeare play?"

Teagan nodded. "The cast plays a theater group that's performing 'The Taming of the Shrew' by Shakespeare – except with songs, of course. As the lead, I play the actress Lilli and character Kate – who is the shrew. I'm really looking forward to the 'shrew' part of my role. In case you hadn't noticed, sarcasm is sort of one of my gifts."

Ida laughed out loud. "Hadn't noticed a bit. So tell me about this double role, then. What kind of characters are Lilli and Kate?"

Teagan spent the new few minutes sharing the basic plot with Ida.

"I'm not sure about how I feel about the last scene where Kate comes out all submissive and sweet – but it's not so much from admitting that she's inferior as much as recognizing that she's met her intellectual match in Petruchio, and by playing the game in front of others they have this respect and freedom that more traditional couples don't have."

"Sounds like you've got that character down quite well already," Ida pointed out.

"Well, ask me that again when I have to kiss him at the end. I have NO idea how

that's going to go." Teagan saw the perplexed look.

"A beautiful girl like you, and you've never been kissed?" Ida inquired.

Teagan laughed. She sensed that Ida would not react like so many other old people, who usually replied with "oh, it's just a phase. When the right one comes along everything will be different."

"Not even close," she replied. "It's not just that I haven't had a boyfriend. I mean, there's been a little interest over the years. But I don't have any desire or attraction in any way for romance, or God forbid, what might come along with that. I don't know how aware you are of today's terminology, but I identify myself as both asexual and aromantic. Have you heard of either of those?"

Ida looked at her for a long moment, and she reached out and took her hands.

"You know, my dear," she began gently, "even though different phrases come and go over time, some things haven't changed as dramatically as everyone seems to think."

Teagan cocked her head to the side, not understanding.

Ida continued, "Even in my day, when one was expected to get married and be a good wife – and it really was the only way to have security – it didn't always mean that marriages were all the same."

"I'm not sure I understand what you're saying."

"Well, even though I loved my husband for providing for me, and I was a good wife when I absolutely had to be, the reality was that the physical part of marriage was something I abhored most of the time."

Teagan stared at her, the realization slowly sinking in. "Do you mean that you were asexual, too? I mean, even getting married and everything?"

Ida nodded. "I know you think that asexuality is a new thing, but it's been around for a long time – even if it hasn't been talked about much. There are some pretty famous people throughout history that are suspected to have been uninterested in sex."

"I know I read somewhere that Edward Gorey was thought to have been ace, but I haven't really heard about anyone else."

"Well let's face it – it wasn't something folks talked about back then. But various writings indicate a strong possibility that Emily Bronte, H.P. Lovecraft, George Bernard Shaw, Nikola Tesla, and J.M. Barrie were possible asexuals. There were others as well if you do the research."

Teagan sat there taking it all in. "I had no idea. God, it makes me feel a little more normal."

Ida gave her hand a squeeze. "I agree. But it's even better to finally MEET someone that understands."

All of sudden Teagan was full of questions. "Was your husband okay with it?"

"He was as supportive as he could be, but there were times when he asked for the attention that I had no desire to give. Granted, that's how Eliana came along, and I'm forever grateful for that, but I'd be lying if I said that I wasn't thrilled when he stopped asking."

"And….you stayed married? And it worked? Even without…."

"The sex?" Ida said with a smirk. "It's okay, my dear, you can say the word. Yes, we stayed married – happily, I might add – until he died. I suspect he might have had a mistress or two along the way, but he was affectionate and caring and seemed to understand my lack of desire. I loved him as a dear man – just not physically. And it all worked out."

Teagan was captivated by all she'd learned. "Thank you so much for sharing all this. You have no idea how much it means."

Ida smiled and patted her hand. "Oh, I think I do," she replied, "because I know that most people truly don't understand, and when you find one that does, it means the world. To BOTH of them."

Just then, Charlotte stuck her head in the door.

"There you are, Ida," she said. "Just wanted you to know that everyone's down for dinner but you. Do you need a push?"

Teagan glanced at the clock and realized that her dad had been outside waiting for a few minutes. "Oh, my!" she said. "I'm sorry to make you late for dinner!"

Ida smiled back as she nodded toward Charlotte for the push. "Not to worry, my dear. It was well worth the extra time! Now you head home, and I'll head down to dinner. And I'll look forward to the next day that you're back to work."

Teagan watched as Ida was wheeled away, loving the older woman all the more. As she grabbed her purse and headed out to meet her dad, she found herself humming the tune to "I Hate Men" all the way to the car.

CHAPTER 11

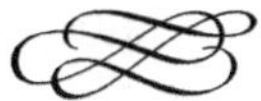

The next few days were busy ones for Teagan, as she had a choreography rehearsal on Thursday and a final paper due on Friday. She had a moment of anxiety as she handed her paper in, knowing that she had committed herself to talking about anorexia and Joanne's death when the oral presentations came around in January.

Teagan spent Saturday morning helping her mom wrap a few Christmas presents, and then decided to ride her bike up to the cemetery since it was Joanne's birthday.

"Are you sure you want to ride? It's cold out there today," her mom said.

"It's cold, but the road's are all clear. I know it might snow later tonight, and then my bike gets put away until spring. I think it will be good to clear my head today."

Her mom came over and kissed her forehead. "You're such a loyal friend to her, my dear," she murmured. "I'm sure Joanne wishes she could do it over again."

"Me, too, mom," Teagan replied as she put on her coat. "I won't be too long."

The cold air felt wonderful as she rounded the corner and crossed the creek. The wind was blowing just hard enough to make the leaves scurry across the road and her eyes water up. The cold kissed her cheeks and her chest almost hurt a bit as she was breathing a little harder than normal. As she was heading in to the first lane of the cemetery, she stopped short as her eyes looked on toward the other end of the cemetery where Joanne's grave was.

"What the hell is SHE doing here?" thought Teagan, as she spotted Cassie jogging down the opposite lane and leaving the cemetery at the other end. She watched her turn left and head down toward Caldwell Manor, and realized that she had seen her jogging here once before.

"That's why she looked so familiar at auditions," Teagan thought. *"I'd seen her here that time and didn't make the connection."*

As she rode down the lane toward the concrete angel, she wondered if Cassie might have a relative buried here as well. She remembered that Brian had said she had just moved here, so that made no sense to her, so maybe she lived near enough to run here.

"She must live in that new development up across from Caldwell Manor," Teagan surmised. *"That's why she headed that way. Probably one of those new huge houses."*

As she approached Joanne's grave, she forgot all about Cassie. Today was her best friend's birthday, and she hadn't missed coming up to visit since her death three years prior.

She sat for awhile on the little stone bench that the Newton family had placed near her grave, feeling the cold against her face as geese flew overhead for warmer winter homes.

"Happy birthday, bestie," she whispered to the name on the stone. "I miss you so friggin' much, but I know you're still here with me. And I admit I feel more peaceful this year because I was finally able to do what you asked me to do. And I sure wish you could be home tonight when Brian and I come for dinner."

Teagan spent the next twenty minutes walking around the grave and telling Joanne all about the first week of rehearsals. Some might think she was loony coming to the cemetery to talk out loud to a piece of granite, but Teagan always felt Joanne's presence here, and today she felt more peace than sadness as she talked to her friend.

Before leaving, she had a thought, and turned one last time to talk to the concrete angel on top of her gravestone. "Joanne, I know that you've seen that girl here – the one that was jogging through when I arrived? I'm worried about her. Maybe I'm crazy, but I'm seeing signs that she might be heading down the same path that you got trapped on. And even though I don't like her, I feel like I need to help her – or at least try. So thanks in advance for any help you can send along, okay?"

With that, she turned her bike away, and looking one last time with love at the name on the stone, she turned and headed for home.

Later that afternoon, she met Brian at the bus stop corner and they walked down Monroe Drive away from Teagan's house. While hers was two away from the bus stop to the east, the Newton house sat two houses away to the west. Brian was in the second block to the south down School Street. As kids they used to think it was a big deal that they were all "two" something away from the bus stop. Every year for as long as they could remember, they headed to the Newton home on this date to celebrate Joanne's birthday, Brian's belated birthday, and Christmas. Even after Joanne's death, they'd kept the tradition alive.

As they approached the house, the first snowflakes of the season began to fall, and Teagan twirled around with her arms toward the sky.

"Brian, look! It's snowing!"

Brian, who wasn't as excited about the upcoming cold weather season, stopped and pulled his hoodie over his head. "Might be a chilly walk home later."

She gave him a playful shove. "Seriously? The first snow fall of the season – on Joanne's birthday, nonetheless – and you're already complaining? I hope we get a FOOT just to spite you."

"Teags, I'm kidding! I think it's beautiful, honest. And hate to disappoint you, but they're just calling for a dusting tonight. And now that we're actually here, do you think we should ring the bell instead of standing out in the snow?"

Teagan smirked and rang the bell, looking back at him. "I owe you a snowball in the face as soon as there's enough to make one."

Beth answered the door, and then Joanne's dad Blake came in from the den.

"Two of my favorite people!" he said as he took their coats. "Glad you could both come."

"Mr. Newton, where else would we be? Then again, Teagan debated skipping dinner to dance in the snow out on your lawn." Brian said with a grin.

Blake Newton chuckled. "Well, knowing how much this one loves the cold, I take that as a huge compliment."

Teagan gave him a hug. "Brian's right about the first part, though," she said. "This is exactly where we're supposed to be on the 20th of December. How are you, Mr. Newton?"

"As good as I can be on this date, I guess," he replied.

They heard a voice yell out from the kitchen.

"You two get in and give your momma a hug, you hear me?"

They both laughed and headed to the kitchen, knowing that they'd find Cheryl Newton with her apron on and finishing up whatever meal they were having. She opened her arms wide to hug them both together.

"You two need to come by more often that just this one night of the year…..you both look great."

"Thanks, Mrs. Newton," Brian replied.

"Excuse me? Mrs. Newton?" said Cheryl, placing her hands on her hips and looking tough.

"Sorry, Momma C!" he said with a smirk, "It *has* been awhile."

Teagan smiled warmly at Joanne's mom. "The house smells divine, Momma. What have you made?"

"Well, I don't know about divine, but it's Chicken Parmagiana – one of Joanne's favorites. I actually managed to get the recipe from Gino himself this week. When I told him it was Jo's birthday he ran right into the kitchen and grabbed it for me."

"Hmmmm," Brian said, rubbing his stomach. "Gino's chicken parm is the best around – I think I eat it at least once a month!"

Teagan nodded. "He does. Only thing he eats more is their pizza. It's almost as if Gino knows that we're some of his most loyal customers or something. So, is there anything I can do to help with dinner?"

"No! Just go and sit for about ten minutes and we'll be all set to eat."

They joined Beth and Joanne's dad in the den as they were watching the last few scenes from the movie Independence Day. As Mr. Newton reached for the remote to turn it off, Brian stopped him and sat right down.

"Hey – you don't turn off the greatest Christmas movie ever right at the end!"

Teagan scooted next to Beth on the other couch and gave her hand a squeeze. "That's Brian for ya! He will forever call this the best Christmas movie."

Mr. Newton nodded in agreement. *"Absolutely!"*

They all watched the end; Teagan could hear Mrs. Newton walking about the kitchen and knew she was getting food on the table. Like clockwork, she called them all in as the final credits were playing.

The meal had always been one of Joanne's favorites, and this year was no exception. The table was laden with platters of chicken parmagiana, penne pasta, salad, and garlic breaksticks. Even the red and white tablecloth reminded Teagan of Gino's, and in no time their plates were full and they were enjoying the meal. Shortly after they began eating, Mr. Newton raised his glass and asked everyone to do the same.

"Here's to you, Joanne," he said, "we will forever love you and forever miss you." His voice cracked a bit as he finished, and everyone else got teary-eyed as their clanked glasses.

"To Joanne," they all said in unison.

"And to promises kept," Brian added, winking over at Teagan as he clanked her glass.

Teagan took a long swallow of water as her emotions settled back down. She missed her friend so much, but gave thanks for the ability to sit with those that loved her as she did.

"Momma C", Brian said, taking another bite of a breadstick, "are these Gino's recipe as well? They're *so* good."

Cheryl Newton laughed. "Not his recipe – just his actual breadsticks. I picked up a couple of orders earlier today and stuck them in the oven to heat up."

Brian took another bite and sighed. "This meal is the best possible way to end the week. Come to think of think of, I started the week with Gino's as well. We had pizza at the read through on Monday."

With that, the conversation turned to the show, and Beth joined in the conversation just as avidly as the two older teens. Teagan sat back and took a sip of her water. *"This really DOES feel like old times,"* she thought. *"It's just a different Newton jumping into the conversation now."*

Cheryl Blake asked if anyone wanted any more food, and Teagan groaned, putting her hand on her stomach.

"Oh, Momma, that was just SO good, but I couldn't eat another bite."

Blake Newton got up and kissed his wife affectionately on the cheek, and said he'd be in his office for a bit, waving at both Teagan and Brian as he headed down the hall.

Brian narrowed his eyes a bit and licked his lips, as though he were considering a third helping. He finally pushed his chair back with a sigh. "I concede. Much as I could easily finish off another serving, I think my body might hate me later on when I'm trying to sleep. Mrs. Newton, that was the best birthday dinner I've had here yet. Only thing that would have made it better is if Joanne were here to join us."

Mrs. Newton nodded wistfully.

"Why don't the three of you head into the den for a bit. I'm going to get the food put away, and then a bit later we can have cake."

Teagan's eyes lit up. "Cake? Did I hear cake?"

Brian poked her playfully. "You just said you couldn't eat another bite!"

Teagan poked him back. "Honey, there is ALWAYS room for cake." She turned her attention to Mrs. Newton. "Do you need some help with dishes?"

Joanne's mother shook her head. "No, but thank you. Just hearing the two of you laughing in the other room will be all the help I need. I know how much Beth misses having her adopted siblings around."

"We love her, too," Teagan answered. "And I think we need to make a better effort to get over here or take her out from time to time."

Beth and Brian had already started toward the den, but Teagan lagged behind for a moment longer. "Momma, how is she doing? It must have been so hard adjusting to being an only child as a 5th grader."

Cheryl nodded, wiping a tear from her face. "It was hell on all of us that first year – not that it isn't still as times. But if Beth hadn't started therapy right away I'm not sure she would have made it.:

"I totally get that. Therapy saved me, too. Well, that and my job. That gang helped me to laugh again. Does Beth have other support?"

"She has a couple of really good friends, and they were her rock – along with you and Brian. I know you don't feel like you get here enough, but know that just by still being a part of her life means the world to Beth. She was always afraid that you'd think she was just the tagalong little sister, and would forget all about her after Joanne's death. Nights like this," she paused a moment, gesturing at the spread on the table, "are the only way I think Beth would get through her sister's birthday."

Teagan could feel her own eyes welling up, and she knew that Joanne's mom wasn't far behind, and she sensed that her second mom would prefer some time alone, so she gave her a quick hug, wiped her eyes, and headed toward the den to join the others.

Beth was chatting about some of the boys in the show, and she mentioned a sophomore that was also in the ensemble. Teagan sat down next to Brian on the couch as Beth had grabbed the "comfy" chair that Joanne always claimed.

"His name is Pete," she said with a smile. "Do you know who I mean, Teagan? He's kinda tall with black curly hair?"

Brian interrupted. "Oh, the one who was in 'Too Darn Hot' with me the other day!"

Beth nodded energetically. "That's him!"

Brian smiled. "I'll have to put a good word in his ear about that cute freshman dancer." Beth's face got all flushed, and Teagan could tell that she really liked this Pete a lot. The younger girl turned to her and inquired,

"So, Teagan, is there anyone that's caught your eye at all?"

Brian glanced sideways and winked with an understanding smile.

"Can't say that anyone has, Beth," Teagan replied. "And you know me; I'm not really in it to meet anyone. I just want to do the show and make Joanne proud."

"But maybe that will change with one of the guys in the show. Maybe even Mike," referring to the guy playing Fred and Petruchio. Teagan thought for a moment, and decided that it was time to open up to Beth. Joanne had always been accepting of Teagan identifying as ace / aro, and she sensed that Beth would be as well.

"I don't see that happening, Beth," she began. "Have you ever heard of asexuality or aromanticism?" When Beth shook her head, she continued. "Well, just like in almost every other species, there are some humans who just seem born without any physical or romantic attractions or desires of any kind. And while some people might expe-rience those feelings from time to time, a person who is ace or aro usually won't."

"Ever?" Beth asked.

"I've basically known I was both since I was about 13 years old. And I don't think I'm going to be one of those that 'grows out of it' when the right one comes along. I just don't see a partner or spouse in my future."

Beth nodded with understanding. "Thanks for telling me. She didn't seem bothered by a lack of romantic interest at all; she just turned her attention to Brian with the same question. He answered with a mischievous grin and a twinkle in his eye.

"I have to admit the guy that plays one of the gangsters is kinda hot. His name is Lou, and he's in my geography class, too. Since rehearsals started he seems to say hi more often." He grinned at Beth and added, "I'll keep ya posted."

Teagan raised her eyebrows at this first mention of an attraction.

"Hmm," she said, "maybe you'll have to 'Brush Up Your Shakespeare' a bit," referring to a song that Lou would sing in the show.

Beth got up and twirled about the room laughing.

"And if things go really well, then I guess Brian will have lots of motivation for his big scene." She started in on the song "Too Darn Hot", and added some jazz moves as she danced and sang. Teagan watched her with amazement. In so many ways she was just like her older sister, but in terms of performing, she had even more talent, and a natural stage presence. She'd be one to watch as she traveled through her high school theater years.

Next Beth switched gears and started singing one of Cassie's songs as Bianca, and Brian got up and joined in as one of her suitors. Teagan couldn't believe it.

"Beth, they just learned that choreography two *days* ago, and you're not even in the scene, but you have it down perfectly! What's with *that?*"

Beth smiled. "Miss Colleen at the studio says that I have a photographic memory when it comes to dance. Go through a routine once for me, and I can usually take it from there. It's like it just comes out of me when the music starts."

Brian patted her on the head. "Well, kiddo, that talent is gonna take you far. And Cassie better watch out. Her understudy might just jump in and take over. God knows you know the dance better right now."

Beth gave him a playful push. "Understudy. I wish." She tapped her finger against his chest and continued, "But mark my words, someday I'll be up there doing a role like Cassie or Teagan. You just wait."

Teagan chimed in. "I have no doubt about that. God, Beth, you're talented, and I think it will get noticed sooner than later. Jeez, I wish it was *you* I was playing against. It would be kinda fun to do that first scene as sisters with you."

Beth's eyes widened with an idea, and she skipped across the room to pick up her script. "Let's *do* it," she said. "Let's read that scene right now. It will be a blast!"

Teagan patted the couch cushion next to her. "Alright, let's. Come sit here, so we can share the script."

For the next few minutes, they read the opening scene between the sarcastic and ill-termpered Kate and her younger sister Bianca, who only wanted Kate to wed so that she could choose among her many suitors. However, she blamed the situation on Kate and more or less told her that no man would ever *want* to marry her. Teagan loved doing the scene with the kid sister she'd adopted years ago, and at the end she beamed at Beth sitting next to her.

"Wow," was all she could say.

Brian, on the other hand, started clapping and whistling. "Woah, girl! You may only be a freshman, but dang! If they'd heard that at auditions, you'd be practicing for real right now!"

Teagan had to admit that Brian might be right. Beth looked back at her for confirmation. "Do you really think so?" she asked.

"Oh my God, yes!" Teagan replied. "That was awesome! And I think our chemistry is way better than what I have with Cassie."

"Yeah, what is *up* with you two, anyway?" she asked. "I've noticed that she seems super sarcastic with you, and whenever you're together on stage there's this tension that goes way beyond the roles you're playing."

Teagan sighed. "We just hit it off on the wrong foot. Cassie doesn't have any tolerance for fat people, and gives the impression that she's so much better than anyone who *is* fat. After callbacks things got a little heated and she started in on how fat girls shouldn't be the lead, and I just let her have it. It wasn't pretty – and I'm not proud of it."

"Woah! What happened? She must have been pissed."

Teagan shook her head. "No, I think I hit a nerve. She was really mad for a second, but then looked hurt the next. I tried to apologize, but she stormed out. I think she's written me off."

"Maybe she's just jealous that you got the lead and have so many scenes with Mike."

Teagan hadn't considered that possibility, as her default mentality didn't usually include romantic explanations. Maybe that really was all it amounted to, and her concerns about Cassie and an eating disorder were totally unfounded. She decided that before talking to Beth about the latter, she wanted to be more sure. It would be a sensitive issue for Beth after losing her older sister, and she didn't want to create any reminders of all that pain. Especially not tonight, when they were getting through Joanne's birthday and actually having a good time.

Cheryl and Blake Newton interrupted just then, with one carrying a tray with cake, and the other a tray with plates and utensils.

Brian sat up and smiled. "Now that is a beautiful sight to behold," he said, gesturing toward the cake. "Mrs. Newton, you spoil us."

Cheryl Newton put the cake on the coffee table and smiled back.

"Brian, believe me, you and Teagan are the ones that spoil us. We're just always glad to have you here. And this cake is partly for YOUR birthday, too."

Beth jumped up, remembering something. "Wait! I almost forgot!" she blurted out as she headed over to a bag tucked under a corner table. She approached Brian and Teagan with two flat gifts wrapped in shiny silver paper topped with a rainbow colored curly ribbon.

"Merry Christmas, you guys," she said to each as she handed them one. "I know it's not really Christmas paper, but I didn't think you'd mind. Open them quick before we have cake!" She knelt down on the floor between them, obviously excited to see their reaction.

Teagan and Brian ripped them open at the same time, and both just sat speechless for a moment. Teagan held a beautiful picture frame collage of all the shows she and Brian had done together with Joanne, and memories washed over her as the tears fell. Seeing the three of them together in so many magical productions was a bit overwhelming. Teagan looked up at Beth with her lips trembling and her eyes filled with tears.

"This is the best gift I've ever gotten. Thank you – so much."

She looked over at Brian who had a simiar reaction, and he wiped his eyes as he nodded slightly.

"She's right, kiddo. These are amazing."

Beth was teary eyed as well, for she had been a spectator for every performance, and often listened to the three of them practicing beforehand. Even Joanne's parents wept openly, as they, too, were transported back to countless memories of their little girl growing up.

Cheryl Newton seemed to sense the need for a positive distraction. "So, how about we all have some cake." She paused for a moment, and then added, "But if it's okay I think we'll skip the singing again this year."

All agreed, and Beth helped to pass out the pieces. They ate in silence for a minute, each remembering Joanne in their own special way. Teagan savored each bite of cake, letting the chocolate flavors swirl around her mouth with the buttercream frosting. This had been Joanne's favorite cake, and every year had been served for her birthday, much like Teagan always asked for carrot cake.

"This one's for you," she thought as she raised her fork, *"Happy Birthday to the best friend I could have asked for, Joanne."* She wondered if she would miss her forever.

CHAPTER 12

Christmas morning Teagan woke up to the smell of fresh coffee, bacon and cinnamon rolls, and she breathed in deep and smiled. She had a whole day at home and she was so looking forward to lounging on the couch, alternating between reading, watching movies, and napping. Oh, and running lines. She knew she'd have to spend some time with her script, even if it might be a bit of a chore on Christmas.

Although she was snug and cozy under her down quilt, the coffee was persistently calling her name, and the cinnamon rolls would taste best warm. *"Hmm,"* she thought with a smile, *"and there will no doubt be chocolate in my stocking for second breakfast."*

She slowly pulled off her cover, knowing it would be chilly. She slipped her feet into fuzzy blue slippers, and grabbed her thick flannel robe that matched in color and pulled it on. She loved that it was a size 3X, as it truly enveloped her entire body with warm flannel, and the tie was long enough to tie in a loose knot and still hang down by her knees. *"No more stingy robes that open when I sit down and have short little ties that hardly stay fastened."* It had been a gift from her parents last year, and was definitely one of her favorites.

She pulled her quilt back up over her pillow haphazardly and headed down to the kitchen. Her mom and dad sat at the table, coffee in hand, chatting quietly. Teagan could hear Nat King Cole's velvety voice singing about chestnuts and Jack Frost, and she knew the morning would be filled with holiday tunes from all of her favorite crooners from the 30s and 40s.

"Merry Christmas, sweetie," her dad said, getting up to wrap her in his arms for a hug. "Sleep okay?"

She nodded. "It was heavenly to sleep in. And waking up to this, " gesturing toward the coffee and rolls, "makes it even better. Merry Christmas, Dad." She next hugged her mom, who had filled a mug of coffee and placed it in front of her spot at the table. The three of them sat down and Teagan reached for cinnamon rolls and bacon. It promised to be a great day.

After a relaxing breakfast, the family moved to the living room where the Christmas tree lights twinkled and the faint scent of fresh baked sugar cookies wafted through the room thanks to a big candle in a jar. Assorted gifts in various sizes and shapes were wrapped in festive Christmas wrapping paper and waited under the tree.

Teagan's dad always played "Santa", and as Teagan and her mom sat down he donned his Santa hat and proceeded to pass the gifts out until each had a small pile in front of them. From the hooks by the hearth he carefully removed three stockings, now overflowing with more wrapped goodies, and added one to each pile.

Teagan loved this part of Christmas much more now than as a child. She remembered wildly ripping paper off of gifts and flinging bows up in the air as her parents watched with contented smiles. Back then she would always finish first, and often missed her parents opening their gifts. Now that she had grown up, they alternated one by one. It took a couple of hours, but each gift got special attention, just like the person opening it.

She chose one that she knew was a DVD from the shape, and smiled at her dad. "You always pick out a good one," she said as she carefully unwrapped the video. She laughed out loud when she turned it over to see that he'd bought her "Kiss Me, Kate".

"I thought you might like your own copy instead of having to hit the library all the time," he explained. She beamed at him and held the DVD close.

"Thanks – I love it! And I'll try not to drive you crazy with it by the end of the day!"

Her mom then opened a beautiful sweater from her dad, who had picked up a gift that Teagan knew was from Brian. They had walked into town earlier that week after school and shopped at the book store and the homemade craft shop, Brooke's Treasures. Her dad read the tag and grinned.

"Brian always gets the greatest gifts," he said as he slowly opened the bag. Inside he found the latest book from his favorite author. "I have my Christmas afternoon planned," he exclaimed. "Brian never fails to disappoint."

Teagan nodded in agreement as she opened a box from her mom. Inside she found two tunic style tops that she'd been eyeing on Amazon for weeks. She smiled at her mom.

"How did you know these two were the ones I wanted most?" she asked as she held the soft, silky material in her hands.

Her mom chuckled. "Brian never fails to disappoint," she repeated. "I knew you'd been looking at them, and I figured he knew which ones you like the best."

Teagan held them up, admiring the greens and blues on black. One reminded her of fireflies on a dark night, while the other had a swirling pattern that brought to mind Van Gogh's "Starry Night" painting. She already knew they would fit, as her parents always got the right size. Teagan thanked her mom, and pointed to a colorful bag with red and green polka dots. "Open that one – we might as well keep singing Brian's praises!"

Peg O'Sullivan laughed, and opened her gift. Inside was a soft fleece scarf that matched her winter coat, as well as a new candle from Brooke's Treasures. She opened the lid of the jar and inhaled slowly. "Hmm......gingerbread," she said. "It's heavenly." She passed the candle to each of them, and her dad took an extra whiff.

"This is always one of the best smelling houses on the block thanks to Brooke. Her candles always smell good enough to eat!"

Teagan laughed, nodding in agreement. They especially loved Brooke's candles because the scent was never overpowering, but truly brought the smells to life as if the item were in the room.

They all opened a few more gifts, and then Teagan found a flat box with a tag from her aunt Carol. She sighed, looking over at her mom. "I wonder what it's gonna be this year?" Her aunt always brought gifts with her when she came for Thanksgiving, and Teagan couldn't remember one that had she had liked or been able to enjoy. She had a tendency to buy clothing that was at least two sizes too small, or other gift items that were juvenile themed and not all something Teagan liked.

This year was no exception. "Really?" Teagan said, shaking her head, already annoyed. Her parents froze, knowing that Teagan was often a little outspoken over her aunt's gifts.

"She got me a subsription to Weight Watchers magazine," she said sarcastically, "with a little note that says 'I hope you'll find lots of tips and recipes that will help you in the year ahead. Always believe in your goals!'" She dropped the magazine and the box on the couch with a shake of her head.

"You know, the gift itself doesn't bug me horribly, because she always buys me things that more or less say 'You're too fat, and you need to diet', but the whole diet industry is what makes me crazy, because they makes billions of dollars a year, and often it just results in women hating themselves and feeling shame over their body size. God, that infuriates me!"

Her dad, always one of her biggest supporters, said to her, "Maybe you'll be one of the ones who helps to change those prejudices. Lord knows the world could use more like you."

Teagan took a deep breath and sighed, giving herself a moment to let it go and calm down. She sometimes doubted that the world would ever accept fat people in the same way that the "young and the gorgeous", Brian's term for thin people, were. One of the gifts of therapy the past several years had been a strengthening of her own positive feelings for her size. While she had always been optimistic, she still sometimes felt the sting of society's prejudices against fat people, but now it wasn't so much something that made her feel inferior as angry that others were made to feel that way.

Her mom gave her an understanding smile. "You can always bring it to work and leave it out – you know several there would love it."

"I suppose," Teagan answered. "Although I'd rather stick it right in the recycling bag so that I don't give the damn magazine a chance to further the bias in someone else's head."

Her dad nodded. "Yeah, I vote that we stick it!"

Teagan laughed. She loved her dad. Not only did he get it, but he also picked up on her subtle barbs. He was going to absolutely love watching her as Kate in the show. As she picked up her last gift to open, she noticed her mom and dad glance at each other, and her dad's wink at his wife. The box was medium sized and wrapped in blue paper with snowmen grouped together like Christmas carollers.

"Hmm....did you get me my own toaster?" she asked with a grin. As she opened the box, her expression was perplexed. "What the...." It was then she realized what lay ahead. Inside was another box, all wrapped in the same paper, and inside that were four more boxes of decreasing size. As she went to open the next, she laughed. "It's like those Russian stacking dolls, but with cardboard instead. And now I'm thinking that maybe you got me my own butter knife to use with the toaster we already have."

Inside the next box was a long and thin silver box, signaling what she hoped was the last one. As she opened it, she squealed with delight and jumped up to hug her parents. "Are you kidding?" she exclaimed. "You got me tickets for Hamilton the Musical?!"

For the past year it had been at the top of her favorites list, and tickets for the Broadway show had been through the roof. Now that it was touring, prices were not quite as high, and it was coming to Boston later in the spring. She still couldn't believe it, hugging her folks a second time. "This is the BEST Christmas present I have EVER gotten!"

Her dad grinned. "I bet Brian will agree with you!" he said, knowing that Brian was an even bigger fan and was the one who convinced Teagan to give the rap style a chance.

Teagan's eyes opened wide and she stopped short.

"Oh, my God! I have to call him right now! Thank you SO much, mom and dad – I love you!"

With that, Christmas morning festivities came to an end. As Peg and Rich cleaned up the assorted boxes that had been discarded, they chuckled at the sound of Teagan's animated conversation coming from the kitchen.

Later that day Teagan's mom drove her over to Caldwell Manor and dropped her off for a couple of hours. She was a favorite employee, partly because she always volunteered to work for a few hours on every holiday. Today she just planned on a Christmas singalong and a few individual visits. She had cards written out for all 32 residents, and some small gifts for a few favorite residents. At the top of that list was Ida, and she looked forward to spending a few minutes with her at some point during the day.

It was quiet at the Manor; some of the residents had gone out with family members for an outing, and others were in their rooms with family that had stopped by for a short visit amidst the holiday burst of activities. For those that had neither, the staff and other residents at Caldwell Manor had become "family," and most were thrilled to see Teagan arrive.

Charlotte and a few aides helped to get residents down to the activity room, and soon the songs of the season filled the room with music and laughter. Teagan always got conversations started after every couple of songs to encourage reminiscing of Christmas stories from long ago. While a few residents wanted to complain about family who didn't come to see them, most chose to share funny incidents of celebrations from their childhoods.

Her favorites – Kitty, Melvin, Gladys, and Ida—were all there, and it made her day more special to have them in it. As residents were putting instruments away, Kitty was still dancing and humming. "You know," she said, "some people would think you were a very strange young lady, choosing to spend your holidays with a bunch of old people."

Gladys poked Kitty from behind. "Hey, who you calling old?"

Teagan hugged them both, whispering "I'll be by to find you both – I have a little something for each of you."

Kitty hugged her back. "Woo hoo! Can hardly wait! And you can find me in the library – that's where I'm heading. Gladys, you coming?"

Gladys nodded, winking at Teagan. "I guess I can go hang out with one of the old people, too." They headed off down the hall, bantering as they went. She noticed that Melvin had already left, but she knew she'd find him down in lobby lounge where he always sat to greet people.

Ida had lingered behind, and she sat in her wheelchair smiling at Teagan. She had pulled a small shiny box out from a sweater pocket, and Teagan knew it had to be for her.

"Ida Vassilikas, what did you do?" she said, smiling at her friend.

"For you, my dear," Ida said, outstretching her hand with the box. Teagan went to her and sat down in the chair beside her. The box was a plain gold cardboard jewelry box with a small bow on top of it. Inside was a beautiful pin with detailed green leaves around the outside. It was in the shape of an olive tree, but this one had a small beaded owl sitting in the tree. Teagan could tell that it was an older pin, but absolutely loved the intricate design.

"This is so exquisite," she said affectionately. "Was it yours?"

Ida nodded. "I got that as a young teen just before we left Crete. Olive trees are everywhere over there, and I always loved owls, so it was a perfect souvenir."

Teagan eyed her older friend with love. "Are you sure, though? Don't you think your own daughter would want this instead? Or even your grand-daughter?

Ida scowled. "Cassandra? No, my dear, her tastes are much more modern – and expensive. And Eliana is not a jewelry person at all. Besides, I want YOU to have it. You love to read, and you're wise beyond your years. That's what makes the owl a perfect symbol for you. And then add in the olive tree, and you have something from my life – sort a perfect friendship pin." She seemed pleased with herself to have come up with a name for it.

Teagan studied the owl and fingered the beading slowly. "I'll treasure this," she murmured. "Just like I treasure you. And before I let you leave, I have a little something for YOU, even if it's not quite as sentimental."

She reached behind the chair and grabbed her bag, and reached inside to find Ida's box. Inside Ida found a beautiful shawl, hand knit with the softest yarn she had ever felt. The primary color was grey, with pastel flowers along the borders.

"I know how chilly it can get in here," Teagan explained, "especially later in the day. I saw this down at a shop in town called Brooke's Treasures. The owner made this herself, so I vouch for the quality."

Ida held it up to her cheek. "The yarn is so soft. And the colors are perfect. Please, can you help me wrap it around my shoulders now? And Teagan," she said, grabbing hold of both hands, "the greatest blessing of moving here has been to call you friend."

"Ditto," Teagan said, as she lovingly wrapped the shawl around her friend's shoulders. "Now, where would you like me to drop you off? I still have to go and deliver a few gifts and cards before my mom comes to get me."

"How about the library?" Ida directed. "I'm almost done with my current book and they have such a lovely selection. Besides, I enjoy listening to Kitty and Gladys go at each other. They really are such great friends." Teagan agreed as she pushed Ida down the hall.

The next morning Brian called early. "Hey, Teags, whatcha doing today?"

She yawned, sitting in sweats on her couch going over lines. "Hadn't made any plans. But aren't you at work?"

"I get off at 2:00 today," he replied. "One of the cast was in this morning and said that some of them are heading over to the Brentwood Mall this afternoon to shop a bit and then grab a bite at the Chinese buffet. They said we should come along. You game? My mom said she could drive us over."

Teagan looked at the clock, which read almost 11:00. While she loved the idea of a quiet day at home, she thought maybe she should get to know a few cast members better. Besides, they had invited her, and that was more than she expected when she first auditioned.

"That works for me," she answered. "And I'll check with my mom. Maybe she or my dad can pick us up so your mom doesn't have to wait around."

"Sounds good, Teags," Brian said. "Look, my break is just about over. See you shortly after 2:00."

Teagan carried her script with her to the kitchen, thinking she should have something to eat for lunch before getting ready. Her mom was sitting at the table with her laptop, but closed it down when she saw her daughter.

"Hey, how goes the memorization?" she asked.

Teagan placed the script on the table, and then proceeded to the refrigerator where she pulled out some leftover turkey and the mayonnaise. She placed them on the counter where a loaf of bread lay waiting for turkey leftovers.

"Not too bad, at least with Act One," she answered. "I should be in pretty good shape with act one when we go back. Second half still needs some work. Hey, Brian called, and some of the cast are heading over to the Brentwood Mall today to hang out and then eat at the buffet. Brian's mom is going to pick me after he gets done at the library. Any chance you or dad could come to get us so she doesn't have to come back?"

"That works perfectly," her mom said. "I know Dad wants to exchange the sweater your Aunt Carol gave him, so you can call when you're heading to dinner, and we should be done by the time you're ready to go. Sound good?"

Teagan took a bite of her turkey sandwich and nodded. "Perfect."

Her mom laughed. "The schedule or the sandwich?"

Teagan grinned. "Both."

A few hours later, Brian honked when he and his mom arrived. He was behind the wheel when she got out to the car.

"Is it safe?" she joked, climbing into the back seat.

His mom laughed. "He's actually a great driver. I'll even trust him to take you out and about when he finally gets his license." Brian flashed his mom a smile and winked at Teagan in the rear view mirror.

"Buckle up, Teags. I'll try to take the corners on all four wheels."

They chatted a bit as Brian drove over to the next town. While Caldwell was quaint and small and hadn't really changed at all over years, Brentwood had "modernized" with the times, adding a mall, several fast food restaurants, a bowling alley, and a movie theater. It was the place to go for anyone in Caldwell who needed a little excitement. Needless to say, that was the bulk of the Caldwell teenagers and young adults on any given weekend.

Teagan had never been a shopper, mostly because very few stores catered to fat people. However, she'd heard that a new stop had opened up for plus sizes, and she was eager to check it out.

Brian stopped the car in the fire lane in front of one of the mall entrances so that he and Teagan could hop out and his mom could take over at the wheel. She gave them both a quick hug and climbed into the car.

"Be sure to thank your folks for me for coming to get you," she said.

"Thanks for the ride, mom," Brian said with a smile. "No wild parties while I'm out."

Mrs. Morris laughed. "Hey, I'm heading home for PJs, a little left-over turkey with a glass of wine, and a cheesy Hallmark movie on TV. Life is good, kids. Have a good time."

She waved as she pulled out, and Teagan thought to herself that she could go for that kind of weekend as she got older. Mrs. Morris had never shown any desire to date again after her husband left years earlier, and proved to Teagan that a happy and contented life as a single adult was more than possible.

They headed into the mall, and Brian explained, "Paula said that a bunch were meeting up in front of the Cinnabon place, and then we can all pick a time and place to meet for dinner at the buffet."

"Anyone who wants to meet at Cinnabon is a friend of mine," Teagan said. "Their rolls are to die for – of course, if we're going to a Chinese buffet in a couple of hours, I'll maybe just get those little bite sized rolls instead of the giant one I usually get. Don't want to be full when dinner time rolls around."

"Rolls around? Did you use that pun on purpose?"

She grinned. "No, but I wish I had."

When they arrived, they found several cast members already drinking coffee and munching on various Cinnabon sweets. Teagan ordered an iced coffee and the six pack of mouth sized rolls. Brian ordered a big cinnamon roll and a hot chocolate. They joined Paula and the two guys who played the gangsters, Lou and Jake. At another table the girls in the cast from the dance studio – Julia and Kyleigh -- waved at Teagan. At a third table Teagan could see several sophomores sitting together. She wondered if either Cassie or Mike would be joining them, and almost as soon as the idea crossed her mind she saw them strolling down the mall heading their way.

"So they came together," Teagan thought. *"I wonder if they are actually dating or just friends?"* Mike stopped at the table and high fived the two guys.

"Glad you guys are here. I was afraid I might be the only guy at a mall with all girls."

All three boys laughed, and Paula jokingly said, "There are worse things, Mike."

Cassie stood to his side, and she acknowledged those at the table with a quiet "Hey" before heading over to sit with Kyleigh and Julia. Mike shrugged his shoulders a bit and followed her, with a quick "catch your guys later."

They all chatted about Christmas, where they were in their memorization, and how much choreography they had forgotten over break. As they finished their coffee conversation turned to shopping. Brian told Teagan he was going to head to the music store with the two "gangsters" – Mike chimed in that he'd tag along as well.

The sophomore trio said they were heading off to the Disney store, and that left just Cassie, Julia, Kyleigh, Paula, and Teagan. As they stood awkwardly looking at each other, Kyleigh noticed Teagan's owl pin. "Teagan, that's beautiful. It's so delicate." Teagan fingered it lovingly as Julia and Paula took a look at it and agreed.

Cassie finally glanced over and took a look. She narrowed her eyes and then stared hard at Teagan. "Where did you get that?"

Teagan was taken aback by her harsh tone, and replied coldly, "Ah, it was a Christmas present. Why?"

Cassie just shook her head a bit and almost hissed. "Never mind."

Julia spoke to break the tension and invited both girls to join them. "Um, we're heading down to the boutique store and then probably to the GAP. We can all go together."

Cassie glared at Teagan, and then said to Julia, "Um, those stores only go up to size 16."

Knowing the remark was really for her, Teagan resisted the urge to lash out as she returned the direct gaze right at Cassie.

"Actually, I'm on my way to try out the new store for plus sizes. It's kinda nice that a few stores have actually figured out that fat people also wear clothes and like to spend money on things that look good." She could hear Julia and Kyleigh snicker a bit as she added, "so I'll catch up with you later. I'm a big girl, I can take care of myself."

Paula smiled at her and then turned to the others. "If you guys don't mind, I'll go with Teagan. I suspect I could easily wear a few of the 1X things, and I've been wanting to check out the new store as well."

"Suit yourself," Cassie said as she rolled her eyes. "Come on, you two, let's head out."

Kyleigh waved and flashed them both a sympathetic smile. "Catch up with you at dinner!"

Teagan smiled and waved back. She knew that Julia and Kyleigh wouldn't be swayed by Cassie's dislike of her.

As they strolled in the opposite direction, Paula asked, "So what's WITH her? Can she get any nastier?"

Teagan chose her words carefully. "Part of that is my fault. She said something after callbacks and might not have meant anything by it, but I kinda blasted her. I'm just hoping we can work okay on stage together."

"Still gives her no right to be so damn nasty – there's enough fat phobia in the world."

Teagan found herself defending Cassie. "She's new this year. She might actually be a little insecure about herself. Those are usually the people that lash out."

They got to the plus size store, and Teagan found several things that she loved. Paula was actually a good shopping buddy in terms of size, and she filed that away for future reference. *Could this be the friend I'm supposed to have?*

As Teagan tried to carry on a conversation about music and

movies, she realized that Paula's tastes were vastly different aside from a few movie soundtracks and the musical Hamilton. Paula was all about hip hop and 80s music, and had never heard of some of the performers that Teagan rattled off. *"Maybe JUST a shopping buddy,"* Teagan thought as they headed back to meet the others.

Brian had a huge smile on his face as they all met up by the Chinese buffet. He held up a bag that clearly had a couple of DVDs in it. "Our New Year's Eve entertainment!" he said with a smile. "But it's a surprise!" Teagan grinned – she knew that could mean anything from a B-rated black and white detective film to an action packed animated film, but she suspected that he had picked up at least one musical.

"Can hardly wait," she answered with a smile. New Year's Eve was another night they had spent together for as long as she could remember, and while she knew that could change at some point, she was glad that she never had to worry about making plans or moaning about not having a date for the foreseeable future.

Cassie reclaimed her spot next to Mike as they headed into the buffet, and while they all sat at a big long table together, she made sure that she and Mike were several seats away, sitting on the other side of Kyleigh and Julia. Teagan could still make eye contact with Cassie if she wanted to, but chose to give most of her attention to Paula, Brian, and the gangsters.

At one point, when she was in line to get to some lo mein, she found Lou waiting beside her. "Hey," he said quietly, looking around to see if anyone else from the cast was close by. "I was wondering...... are you and Brian...an item?"

"Ah," she said with a pause, thinking that maybe there was some interest on Lou's part, although she wasn't sure whether it was for her or Brian. "That would be a no. Brian's like my brother. I love him with every fiber in my being, but that's all he'll ever be."

She saw Lou's body relax a bit. "I was pretty sure he's gay, but you guys are together all the time."

"Look," she said, reaching at last for the lo mein, "If you're asking because you might be interested, all I can say is that he's not seeing anyone and I think you should definitely pursue that."

The smile on Lou's face confirmed that her best buddy indeed had an admirer. She winked at Lou as she handed him the tongs, "And now if you'll excuse me, I have a date with General Tso." She looked back as she walked away, and Lou was still smiling as he loaded his plate.

She rejoined the others at the table and couldn't help but smirk at Brian.

"What's that face for?" he asked.

"Nothing," she said back. "I'm just in a good mood all of a sudden. Must be General Tso here", indicating her favorite menu item heaped on the plate before her. Brian just shrugged and took a big bite of his chicken wing. Teagan watched as Lou returned to the table; he was seated across from Brian, and Teagan could sense that Brian was glad to have him there. Paula was seated across from her, and they talked about their favorite foods.

"Always a good topic of conversation for me," thought Teagan to herself. *"I guess if nothing else Paula and I can talk about food."* Her attention drifted down to the opposite end of the table as Cassie returned with her plate. Her heart sank a bit as she watched Cassie sit down. On her plate she could see a few shrimp and a small spoonful of rice. The remainder of the plate had green beans and some other Chinese greens.

Teagan's attention was torn between chatting with Paula and the guys and glancing down the table. She realized that Cassie had seated herself in the perfect spot to be "invisible". The sophomores at the end were chatting amongst themselves, and Mike was talking to Cassie, but also to Jake, who was next to him. There was an empty seat between Lou and Cassie, and Teagan wondered if she hadn't purposely isolated herself a bit. As the meal progressed, Teagan watched Cassie play with her food, rearranging it on the plate. She'd occasionally pick something up with her fork and hold it as if she were going to eat it, and then as Mike's attention went elsewhere she brought the fork back down to the plate and replaced the item with something else.

"Oh, Cassie," she thought, "I wish to God I was wrong, but I don't think I am. But how in the world can I possibly try to reach you if we can't have a civil conversation?" After Mike and Jake got up to go and get a refill, Cassie handed her plate to a passing waitress and sipped her water. As she glanced toward the others, her eyes locked with Teagan's. Teagan knew in an instant she was right. She'd seen that same scared, desperate look in Joanne's eyes the summer before she died. All of sudden Teagan had a new promise to keep.

CHAPTER 14

It was New Year's Eve, and Teagan was dressed for her big date with Brian. Her sweats were the most comfortable clothes she owned, and she loved the fact that she could spend the end of the year in the way she loved most – curled up on a couch under a blanket, watching a movie with her best friend. She grabbed her bag with her laptop, script, and presentation notes and headed down to the kitchen. Her mom had a small bag on the counter and slid it toward her.

"Thought I'd send along a contribution for the evening's festivities," she said smiling.

Teagan peeked inside the bag. There was a plastic container of chicken wings that her mom had made earlier, another with Swedish Meatballs, and a third with something white inside.

"Dip?" she asked, and her mom nodded.

"I did that Ranch dip that Brian likes so much," her mom replied. "There a plastic bag of veggies and another bag of chips to go along with it."

Teagan wrapped her arm around her mom's shoulder and gave her a hug. "You are absolutely the best mom – you DO know that, right?"

Peg O'Sullivan leaned over and gave Teagan's head a kiss. "You make it pretty easy, kid. Now, do you have everything? I have to head down to pick up a bottle of wine for your father and I, so I can drop you off. Are you staying over or planning on coming home after midnight? Dad can zip down to get you if you call."

Teagan shook her head. "I'll just crash on the couch. That's easier for you guys, and Brian's mom usually makes pancakes for breakfast, so that's major motivation to stick around until morning."

Her mom laughed. "Maybe you should call me to come and get you – right around the time those pancakes are hitting the plates. Her pancakes are better than the diner."

"Whose pancakes are better than the diner?" said Teagan's dad as he walked into the kitchen.

Teagan turned and smiled. "Mom thinks that Brian's mom makes the best – and I think she just invited herself down there for breakfast in the morning."

Her dad laughed. "Count me in – although I HAD planned on taking her down to the diner for breakfast since you usually crash elsewhere on New Year's – then we could pick you up on the way home."

Teagan watched her mom give her husband a kiss on the cheek, and then turned to her daughter. "Sorry, honey, tell Mrs. Morris that her pancakes might be great, but breakfast with this guy at the diner wins just for the company."

Rich O'Sullivan flashed a grin at his wife, and then looked at the clock. "What can I say? I've still got it! Now get out of here and have a great time!" He winked at Teagan and added, "and I'll see you next year!"

Teagan groaned and grabbed the bag off the counter, and then her bookbag by the door. As she and her mom headed out to the car she called back over her shoulder. "Love you, Dad! Happy New Year!"

An hour later, Brian and Teagan had heated up the chicken wings and meatballs and loaded their plates for a New Year's Eve feast. Brian's mom had gone to a friend's apartment two doors down to welcome in the New Year by playing board games with a few friends from work, so they planned a double feature movie night with lots of talking and running lines in between.

Brian also removed something from the oven that smelled heavenly.

"Quiche?" Teagan asked, although the scents didn't quite match. It was a sweet smell, but definitely something with cheese.

Brian shook his head. "Another geography project – gonna bring it in for class this week when we go back. It's what people in Bulgaria eat on New Year's, and it's called Banitsa."

Teagan bent down and inhaled slowly. "Hmm, that smells divine. Is that pastry dough?"

Brian nodded as he grabbed a knife and began to cut it. "It's made with phyllo dough layered with eggs and cheese – a little like Panera's souffles." He cut a big piece and managed to squeeze it onto her plate without knocking off anything already piled on it.

Teagan grabbed a fork and took a bite. "I am SO bummed I didn't take that geography class. Those guys have been spoiled rotten by you this year." She took another bite and added, "this is awesome."

As they carried their plates over to the coffee table, Teagan asked, "So what are the surprise movies you bought at the mall?

Brian put his plate down and then crossed to the TV where two DVDs were sitting. He held up the first. "First up is Ghostbusters II – where they save the city on New Year's Eve."

Teagan nodded from her spot on the couch. "Awesome choice – what's the second half of the double feature?"

Brian grinned. "This one is just because we're both dorks. I don't know if any of our peers would get excited." He held up the classic movie by Bing Crosby called "Holiday Inn" and Teagan squealed.

"Oh, my God – I LOVE that movie! Definitely save that for last! And your taste in movies is as good as your baking abilities, I might add."

They actually sat and watched the beginning of the first movie as they ate, interjecting comments along the way about the actors and the plot.

"This is why we should never be allowed to watch movies in a theater," Brian said as he popped a meatball into his mouth.

"Because we never shut up?"

He nodded, chewing with a smirk. "I wonder if I even COULD be quiet through a whole movie at this point…maybe I better practice a bit."

She gave him a sideways glance and noticed him sitting there with a smile on his face. "Wait a minute, did something happen that I should know about?"

He grinned. "If you must know, I got a phone call last night from Lou. We talked for, like, an hour."

Teagan grinned back. "AND?"

"And we're going to a movie next week some time. He seems really nice, Teags."

She squealed. "I *knew* it! I could tell there was some interest at the mall the other day. So what did you guys talk about?"

Brian ran his hand through his hair and sighed. "Everything. Anything. I don't know. We talked about school, and geography, and traveling the world, and theater, and family stuff, and …… like I said – everything, I guess. We have a ton in common. He also loves to cook, and has been wanting to ask me about this geography project of mine since I brought the first thing in to class."

Teagan sat there with mixed emotions. She was excited to hear Brian talk about Lou with a twinkle in his eye and a smile on his face. But realizing that he and Lou might be starting a new friendship that didn't include her as much made her a bit sad.

The other emotion that she felt was a kind of confusion. "*So this is what it's like to feel romantic attraction,*" she thought, listening to Brian talk. While she was happy for him, she knew that the concept of romance would always be a mystery to her.

Her thoughts turned to Paula for a minute. They sure didn't have much in common, but was she the new friend that Joanne had encouraged her to find? Up until now Brian had filled that role, but now she began to understand why Joanne had included meeting others as part of the promise. Sadly, she just didn't feel that Paula would fill that need.

"Hey, Teags, where'd you go just now?" Brian asked. "You were a million miles away."

"Thinking about Joanne," she replied, "and how happy she'd be for you right now." She wasn't ready to share her feelings with him yet; she needed some time to process everything first.

Brian seemed content with that reply, and she noticed he had finished his food and had pulled out his notes for geography class. "Gotta check to see where we're heading next in class and maybe do some research for foods to try." He scanned the syllabus and pointed to the upcoming assignments. "Looks like I need to find something from Northern Europe, and then Southern Europe. I've got this Banitsa from Bulgaria for the Balkan States, so I think I'll find something Scandinavian, and then either Italian or Greek, maybe?"

The mention of Greece gave Teagan an idea. "Hey, I can help there," she offered. "One of my residents grew up on the Isle of Crete – I can ask her about Greek desserts if you'd like." Brian nodded in response. The thought of Ida brought a smile to her face. "I'll have to bring you in to meet her. She is the neatest lady I think I've ever met."

Brian turned to her. "How so?"

"Believe it or not," Teagan began, "she and I had a long conversation about being ace, and she told me what it was like growing up ace in another generation."

"Whoa, you mean an old lady at the Manor identifies as ace?" Brian asked.

"Uh-huh. And she talked about what it was like to be ace in a world where you were still expected – especially as a woman – to get married and have families. It was fascinating to listen to someone who totally gets me, even if she had to live a totally different life because of when she was born."

"I take it she got married, then?"

Teagan nodded in response. "Yeah, but her husband more or less accepted her lack of interest. She still shared a romantic bond, but the physical union was, ah……sparse."

Brian chuckled. "Well put, Teags. Any kids manage to appear?"

She smiled. "She has one daughter whose family now lives in her old house, ovver in Brentwood. God, she's just an amazing lady."

"Sounds like it. And tell her that I'll make her whatever Greek dessert she wants!"

With the topic back onto Brian's geography homework, Teagan pulled out the binder with her health class project notes. "Now if only THIS assignment could be as wonderful as yours."

"That your anorexia project?"

She nodded as she scanned through her notes. "I turned in my paper and I have no doubt I'll do fine on that. But this damn oral presentation is making me crazy. I'm trying to organize some basic notes but it's almost impossible to do without knowing who my partner is going to be."

"Yeah, I can see that. Any ideas at all what some of the other kids have chosen?"

Teagan shook her head. "I can't say I was paying much attention in class the past few weeks. I guess I can just jot down some bullet points for the key components, and then adapt them as needed once I know. I just hope it's not something like 'healthy dieting' or something. I might need to kill someone."

The finale of the movie was fast approaching and caught her attention. "Hey, Brian, maybe we should at least watch them save the city, since you paid for the movie and all."

He laughed, and for the next few minutes they left their homework behind to watch the Ghostbusters and the Statue of Liberty. "The Pillsbury Doughboy was way better, just sayin'" Brian interjected. Teagan grinned and nodded as they continued watching to the end.

In between movies they got out the dip and prepared a platter of veggies and chips, and then settled down to watch Holiday Inn. Teagan looked at the clock, and estimated that the movie would end just a few minutes before midnight. They'd no doubt switch to the television to watch the countdown in Times Sqaure, and then crash for the night. Teagan was not a late night person, and she'd probably be asleep by 12:15.

As they watched the second movie, they sang along with all the songs, and Teagan wondered if this might be their last New Year's Eve together. If Brian began dating, she might have to figure out what else to do on New Year's Eve. Maybe she'd go up to Caldwell Manor and do crossword puzzles with Ida, or have a singalong and countdown earlier in the evening. Or maybe, just maybe, she'd find someone else to connect with that might be a friend for the future. Time would tell.

CHAPTER 15

A few days later Teagan was heading into the first rehearsal of the new year. She was excited to start really working with her cast mates. Aside from the read through and one music and choreography rehearsal, cast members had been told to memorize their lines over break and be ready to jump right in to blocking.

Teagan was looking forward to most of her scene work today. She had some great sarcastic lines with Mike as they began as Lilli and Fred, and then some physical "shrew" moments as Kate in her opening scenes of the play within a play. The only spots she was nervous about was some romance with Mike in the beginning, and then her opening scene with Cassie when she threatened to hit her with a broom.

She could understand her apprehensions playing the romantic scene, but wasn't sure why she was nervous about her scene with Cassie. They clearly had some great animosity between them, so it should be an easy scene to do. Yet somehow those were the lines she was most nervous about.

At the moment, she was watching her stage "sister" doing her opening song and dance number with her three suitors. Cassie played the role of Bianca flawlessly, and her dancing was amazing. Teagan could almost close her eyes and see Joanne making the same flirty gestures before whirling away to another waiting suitor. Cassie's voice sounded a little tired—as it had in auditions—but her tone was perfect for the role.

"If nothing else," thought Teagan, *"maybe we can find common ground through our love of theater."* Brian had snuck over to sit next to her part way through the song, and whispered sideways to her, "Damn, Teags, she's really good." Teagan nodded in agreement.

She also noted that Lou and Jake had come over to sit next to Brian to watch as well. She smirked and raised her eyebrows in a questioning manner toward Brian. He just winked and grinned back, sitting back in his seat to be able to whisper in the other direction as well. Much as Teagan knew that things might change soon, she could only feel happiness for the one who had pulled her back from the brink three years ago.

As the quartet on stage finished their song, those in the auditorium applauded for them, and Liz Patterson praised them for remembering their dance as well as they had. She then turned to Mr. C. and swept her arm toward the performers. "They're all yours, boss." She turned back to those in the audience and yelled out, "Don't forget – tomorrow we go over all the big ensemble numbers that we practiced before the holiday. I expect that it will just be review and not a whole session of re-teaching – got it?" Her question was met with a few groans, and Teagan knew she meant it. She also knew that in theater every cast member had to give their all and practice outside of rehearsal, or they'd just hold back the entire group. Maybe she'd try to grab Beth during lunch the next day just to refresh her own memory. She surely wouldn't want to be the one who held the cast back by not being as prepared as she could be.

Ann, the stage manager, was now calling her up for the next scene, which was her first scene as Kate. "Okay, listen up," she said as she addressed those on stage. "Just so a bunch of you don't have to sit around waiting, Mr. C. decided to do this scene first with most of you in it, and then work down to the last scene of the day with just those playing Lilli, Fred, Hattie, and Paul. Got it?" Everyone nodded in agreement, and Mr. C. began going through their rough blocking. One shy freshman raised her hand and spoke hesitantly.

"I'm sorry – could you explain what blocking is again?" Amid some snickers and other groans, Mr. C. maintained a calm demeanor and shushed everyone before turning to the girl. "There are no stupid questions here, understand?" She nodded, looking a less apprehensive. "Blocking," he continued, "is the set of directions I'll give you that tell you where to enter from and what to do on stage in terms of movement. And for the record, I'd rather have someone ask me a question than try to come out and fake it. So kudos to you today – and for anyone else that isn't sure of what blocking and stage directions are, I'd suggest you get here fifteen minutes early tomorrow and I'll have Ann go through a little exercise with you to go over it, okay?" Several nodded, and Teagan noted that a couple of the sophomores that had been at the mall seemed to be grateful that someone had brought the subject up.

Mr. C. told her that she'd be up on a small platform in a window for her opening lines, and asked if she'd be comfortable standing on a large wooden block to practice. She nodded to him, and then looked at the portable piece and prayed that it wasn't just cheap plywood. She climbed up onto it and faced the action in front of her. Although it certainly wasn't up high like she'd be in the show, the block gave her a sense of height and made her feel more powerful. Ann brought over a few props that she'd be throwing out at the male members of the ensemble in her opening scene.

"This might be fun," she wondered. Her opening line as Kate was actually a scream, and when her cue came Kate let it out with gusto. Many of the cast turned toward her with their mouths open in surprise at her volume and intensity. Mr. C. just grinned at her and gave her a thumbs up signal. *"This really WILL be fun,"* she thought to herself, and went on with the remainder of the scene having a blast throwing things while screaming.

When it was time for her next scene, Teagan was a little less nervous to face Cassie head on. She began the scene chasing Cassie out the door waving a broom at her, and running after her around a table and back to where Cassie found solace with her father. Teagan's character Kate was jealous of her sister being the favored daughter and angry that she father had refused to let the younger marry until she as Kate found a husband.

When Teagan came out the door with the broom and Cassie turned to plead with her, she sensed that Cassie was truly worried that Teagan would hit her. Teagan knew that she had to be in total control of her ample body as she chased her sister about or she could hurt her. Over the years she had grown confident in what her curves could and couldn't do, and she felt totally sure of every pound she carried on her large frame.

During the second run through, Cassie seemed to relax more into her role, and as their scene began Cassie met her gaze again. This time, however, Teagan saw the character of Bianca looking back. Their chemistry on the stage was perfect, and everyone in the room either nodded or clapped lightly when they finished. Teagan went to pick up her broom, and as she passed Cassie, she smiled at her.

"That was pretty amazing, Cassie. I think for the first time we really clicked."

"Whatever," Cassie said, rolling her eyes as she walked away.

Teagan watched her go. *"This might be harder than I thought,"* she said to herself. She would have liked to follow Cassie and try to have a conversation, but Anne was dismissing those that were finished, and Cassie walked quickly over to Mike and said something to him. Teagan watched him nod, and then she was gone.

The first scene Teagan had with Mike was the one that made her most nervous. She knew that she could handle the sarcasm okay, and she was correct. They were flawless in their dialogue, and Teagan really felt a connection to Mike as they threw insults and saucy barbs back and forth. It was during the song they had to sing when Teagan could feel herself getting stiff and less sure of herself.

All of a sudden they were supposed to be reminiscing about their past love affair and how wonderful it all was. Teagan sang and danced with Mike as directed, and at one point they ended up sitting on the bench with hands clasped, singing to each other, when Mr. C. directed her to swivel around and have Mike wrap his arms around her to finish the song with his face next to hers. She could feel his arms wrap around her and hold her arms in his, and she felt his breath warm on her cheek as he finished the song. She knew her character Lilli was supposed to be enthralled by the memories, and she tried hard to imagine what that was like.

Mr. C. finished up the scene, and asked her stay for a minute to be measured for her costume. She nodded as she saw Hattie and Paul getting measured first. Mike strolled over to her and smiled. "Hey, Teagan," he started, "I sensed that you were kind of nervous for that last song. You felt really tense. Anything wrong? Or am I doing anything to piss you off that I don't know about?"

Teagan shood her head and grinned. "Just a little rusty with the love scenes. I'll get there, don't worry."

Mike flashed her a smile that would probably have made the average girl in the cast swoon inside. "Maybe I can help you a little with that as we go," he said, and Teagan honestly couldn't tell if he was flirting or not. She'd had to ask Brian for advice.

"But for now," Mike continued, "I gotta run. Cassie's outside waiting and we're heading to Gino's." He shook his head a bit and continued, "Although sometimes I wonder why we go out to eat. She hardly ever eats anything while we're out. Just kinda plays with her food and has a few bites, then takes the rest home." He eyed Teagan up and down and smiled a bit. "I bet if I took you to Gino's you'd eat at least a couple of slices, wouldn't you?"

Teagan didn't care if he was flirting or not – he was speaking her language when he brought up Gino's pizza. "Honey, if it was sausage and onion, you might have to fight me for it." And with that she turned and headed over to Mr. C., leaving Mike watching her intently before heading out the door.

Mr. C. and an older lady were waiting for her, and he introduced her as Mrs. Healey, the costume coordinator. "She's gonna measure you a bit, and I'd like to go over a couple of notes at the same time if that's okay." Teagan nodded and raised her arms out to her side as Mrs Healey began to measure her body. She suddenly felt rather self-conscious as she stood there in front of the male director with an old lady wrapping a tape measure around her chest and hips. Mr. C. seemed totally unfazed, however, and picked up his yellow legal pad which he scribbled on throughout rehearsals.

"Overall," he began, "you are nailing this part right from the start. I watched you in auditions and just knew that you had the fire and feisty attitude for this role, and you haven't disappointed me. I think you scared most of the the underclassmen today – can hardly wait to see what you do in performance."

Teagan thanked him softly, grateful that Mrs. Healey had moved on to her thighs and arms at this point.

Mr. C. continued, "The only area I feel like we need to work on is the romance. You seemed to just tighten up a bit today, and I was a little surprised to be honest. That scene with Mike today was superb until you got to the song – and then I didn't see Lilli anymore – I just saw Teagan, who didn't look all that sure of herself."

Teagan nodded sheepishly. "You're spot on, Mr. C." she admitted. "That part of the scene just felt really foreign to me, and I guess I have to find my motivation."

"I get it," he said, gesturing with hand his hands up as if to stop her apology. "Hey, just think back to the first time you've been in love, or even infatuation. I'm sure it's not *that* long ago."

This time Teagan smiled amused.

"What? What did I say?" Mr. C. asked.

"It's just that what you're asking might be a lot harder than you think. You see, Mr. C., I'm asexual."

Mrs. Healey, who had been jotting things down, looked up inquisitively. "A sexual what?" she asked matter of factly.

Teagan stifled a laugh and addressed them both. "No – that's *asexual*. It means that I don't feel any sexual attraction to another person. It's like I miss the normal cues that people use when they flirt. I don't understand because I have never experienced the attraction."

Mrs. Healey smiled sweetly and patted her hand. "Oh, sweetie, that will change when the right one comes along. Don't you worry that pretty little face about it." Teagan looked toward Mr. C., hoping to find a more sympathetic face, and he seemed unfazed.

"Okay, thanks for that. I'll keep that in mind and see how we can work that to our advantage." He then turned to Mrs. Healey and said, "So, what have you got for her?"

Mrs. Healey shook her head slightly, looking at her list of clothing that she had and the list of measurements that she'd just taken with Teagan. Teagan all of a sudden felt very self conscious. Even though she was happy with her size, she could feel the anger rise up inside a bit when she knew she was being judged for being fat. And along with the anger she felt some shame for being fat, which made her even more angry for allowing society to make her feel inferior because of a number on a tape measure.

CHAPTER 16

The next day Teagan sat in health class waiting to hear who her partner would be for the big oral presentation. She was only half listening to the lecture, as she found herself doodling the letters "C" and "J" in the margins of her notebook. Since Mike had talked about Cassie's behavior at Gino's she'd been thinking more of the common behaviors between Cassie and Joanne, and it worried her. If Cassie did have anorexia then she wanted her to get help. At the same time, she had no real connection with her and wasn't sure who might. She feared that Cassie hadn't made any close friends since moving to town, which only made it easier to hide an eating disorder from others. *"Maybe Mike could talk to her, or one of the girls at the studio."*

As the teacher began calling out the names of project partners, she refocused her attention to the front of the room. There were no hints as to what various individual papers had been about, so even after learning her partner's name she wouldn't know for sure what direction the project might go. When she heard her name called, she was somewhat relieved to hear the name Barb Sanders called as her partner.

She'd known Barb since middle school, but only as a classmate.

She'd seen Barb with Cassie at school and wondered if that wouldn't be a useful connection. Teagan smiled across the room to acknowledge their new partnership, and for the last few minutes of class students were allowed to finally find their partners to chat.

"Hey, Barb," Teagan said with a smile, "I'm glad that my partner isn't a complete stranger."

"Me, too," she replied. "I was also really hoping I wouldn't have to work with a guy on this one."

Teagan nodded with understanding. "So, I guess the big question is what two topics are we trying to present that won't sound totally far-fetched together."

Barb look relieved. "Right? That bugged me all break – like what if our topics are totally not complementary? Then what do we do?" She paused a moment and looked around the room, trying to gauge how other pairs were reacting to their topics. She looked back at Teagan and continued. "So my individual topic is on bulimia. My cousin really struggled with it in college this past year, and she said it really started when she was our age. I thought if I could make kids our age more aware it might help."

Teagan smiled, glancing at the teacher who was strolling around answering questions.

"I don't think we'll have any trouble at all. My topic is anorexia, so we're both presenting on eating disorders."

Barb sighed slightly. "Whew! That's a relief; those topics are perfect together. Hey, I know you have a ton of rehearsals now, but are there any days that we could meet at the library after school to plan an outline? I think we can do most of the work on our own once we know how to put the pieces together."

Teagan nodded in agreement. "The library is perfect, and I'm actually free today if you are. That's about the only day this week between rehearsals and work. Otherwise, maybe we could do lunch in the next day or two."

"No, today works," Barb replied. "I just have to text my mom to make sure it's okay."

Teagan knew she would as well, so they both took a minute to contact their moms and exchange cell phone numbers. Teagan knew she could head over right after school with Brian as he was working that day. She asked Barb if she'd like to walk with them.

"Do you mind if I meet you there about half hour later? I don't have my notes with me, and my mom said she could pick me up and dash me home and then drop me off. Where do you want to meet?"

Teagan described "her" spot. "I always sit at the back table of the reference section. It's somewhat out of the main traffic area but still gives you a good view of the room."

"I know just what table you're talking about. I'll see you there."

Teagan texted Brian that she'd be heading to the library with him, and then headed off to her last class. An hour later, they met up outside and made the short walk to the library, and she filled him in on her project partner.

"All that worrying for nothing," he teased, "It sounds like you and Barb are a great match up."

She nodded and brought up the question she wanted to ask him. "So, I need your advice on something. I think Mike might have flirted with me a little yesterday at rehearsal, but I'm not sure……'cause, you know, I don't have a clue about those things. But if he did, then I need to figure out how to gracefully address it. One, because I'm just not into him at all, and two, because he's also sort of seeing Cassie, and I don't need one more thing for her to hold against me."

She relayed the conversation at rehearsal and Brian grinned. "Hate to tell ya, Teags, but sounds like he was hitting on you. Maybe you should just come out to him and let him know who you are. He seems like a good enough guy. And then when Cassie gets all jealous and starts accusing you of trying to steal her man he can back you up."

"Oh, God. Please don't let it come to that. I'm worried about her, and I don't know what to do. We had a real connection for the first time on stage yesterday, but one word about anorexia and she'll shut down fast. I'd love to just stay out of it, but what if I'm the only one who sees it?"

"I'm sure others are seeing stuff, too, Teags, but it doesn't look like anyone is close enough to her to bring it up. Why not talk to that nurse at work again to get her advice. If you go to the school nurse you'll be setting the ball in motion right now, so you might wanna be sure it's the best time."

"Oh, God, she might get pulled from the show. Talk about another reason to hate me."

They arrived at the library, and Brian bid her farewell as he headed off to sign in. Teagan headed over to her spot and looked over her notes until Barb arrived. She was exactly a half hour later, just as she'd said she would be.

"When you say a half hour, you mean it exactly," Teagan said with a grin.

"Punctuality. It's a blessing.....and a curse," Barb joked as she sat down and unpacked her notes. "Got it from my mom, whose philosophy is that she's not on time unless it's ten minutes early."

For the next hour they compared notes and came up with an outline, discussing the best way to present. Barb looked over their preliminary notes and said, "I think we need to open with a quick general overview of eating disorders – not just anorexia and bulimia, but also compulsive overeating. Let's face it, eating disorders can affect *anyone*. Would you agree?"

Teagan nodded. "Absolutely. Then we can each present individually on our separate topics, and then at the end reiterate the need for intervention regardless, and maybe some common red flags to look for?"

"Absolutely. And some resources on where to get information. I know some kids might have questions about where to turn for help."

"That's brilliant," Teagan replied as she jotted things down. "Even better, let's give them a handout. Some kids might not want to talk about it in class."

"I wonder if there's a handout somewhere on how to talk to someone you think might have a problem."

Teagan stopped writing and looked at Barb. "I wish I'd had something like that a few years ago. Maybe it would have made a difference."

Barb looked pensive for a moment. "You're talking about Joanne, right? I remember you guys were always together in middle school. Is that why you picked your topic?"

Teagan's face turned solemn as she nodded. "Yeah. We all knew there was a problem, but I think we approached her wrong. I think we pushed her away instead of getting her help. Maybe a different approach would have helped."

"Hey, from what I know from my cousin, you can't feel guilty about that. There's so much denial involved. *That's* what causes the isolation."

"But I've learned since that there *are* better ways to bring it up. I just wish I could figure out how to use them now…"

Barb's eyes met hers with understanding. "You're talking about Cassie now, aren't you?"

Teagan sighed. "So I'm not crazy? You've seen it, too?"

Barb nodded. "Yeah, I'm kinda worried about her and wonder if she doesn't have a problem. But it's not exactly something that you just go up and say, 'Gee, you seem have a problem with food and exercise. Do you need to go inpatient somewhere before you die?' God, I'm sorry – that probably hit a nerve."

"It's okay. But yeah, definitely not the words to use. I've done a lot of reading since Joanne died, and you can't use the word 'you' when you're talking to them or they get all defensive. You always have to say it from your perspective, like 'Gee, I notice that you're not eating in front of others anymore. I bet that's a little lonely sometimes.' So, Barb, what kinds of things are you noticing with Cassie? 'Cause I've noticed things as well."

Barb looked around, almost as though she was making sure they were out of ear shot. "What you said, about not eating in front of others. When Cassie first moved here she'd hang out with Chelsea and me, and we'd go to a movie or dinner over in Brentwood a whole lot. Cassie would usually do the salad bar, but she'd have pizza sometimes – or even a burger. But lately…..she might order her food like she always has, but she ends up just rearraging it on the plate, and always either offers it to someone else, or gets a doggie bag because she's too full. Which is crap, because she never eats."

Teagan nodded. "I saw the same stuff at our rehearsal read through. I had talked to a friend of mine at work who's a nurse, and she thinks she definitely needs help. I'm actually going to talk to her again this weekend to find out the best way to intervene. I'm not close to Cassie, but I see so many behaviors that Joane used to display, and I couldn't live with myself if something happened to her. Do you know much about her family? Are her parents approachable?"

Barb shook her head. "Never met them. I've see her mom in the car on occasion when we'd go to Brentwood, but she never wanted to carpool. Neither Chelsea or I have ever been to her house, even though it's in the development just down the street – Madison Circle, I think it called?"

Teagan looked perplexed. "Are you sure? I had assumed she lived up at the other end of town in the Manor Drive development. I've seen her up jogging in the cemetery a couple of times, and she headed that way when she was done."

Barb shook her head. "No, I know it's other way, because Chelsea looked it up once. And if she was jogging, she probably just cut back down Lincoln Ave. toward the high school and came around by the library."

"That makes sense," Teagan conceded. "And it's a relatively easy jog, I guess."

She looked at the clock and realized her mom would be there shortly to pick her up.

"Hey, my mom will here in ten minutes, so I guess we should wrap it up. I think we're in a good place on the presentation. I'll send you what I have on powerpoint when I get it finished and you can do the same?"

Barb nodded. "I can put it together if you want. I know how busy you are with rehearsals and work."

"That would be awesome," Teagan admitted. "And I'll keep you posted on where things stand with Cassie after I talk to my nurse friend again. I'm hoping that with a few of us all trying to help we might be able to save her before she gets any worse."

"Hey, just don't set the bar too high; I sense that you're determined to save Cassie as some pay back to Joanne. Remember that you can't help someone unless they admit they need it. I don't know if Cassie is there yet."

"I know. Hell, I don't even *like* her, so I'd love to not deal with this. But something inside just keeps nagging at me to try and reach her."

Barb smiled. "Maybe it's Joanne. She might be trying to tell you that you're the only one that *can* reach Cassie."

Teagan groaned. "God, I hope you're wrong. That's the last thing I wanna go through all over again." Her phone vibrated on the table. "That'll be my mom outside. Thanks for coming, Barb. I think our presentation will be really good."

She grabbed her bag and headed outside, wondering if maybe Barb might be that new friend that Joanne had included in her promise. Because it sure as hell wasn't going to be Cassie Durand.

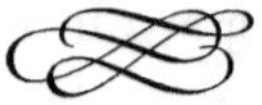

CHAPTER 17

Teagan was truly looking forward to work on Sunday, as she had only been on the schedule one other afternoon all week. Much as she loved being a part of the musical, it definitely took a day away from her favorite people in the world. Her dad dropped her off and she hastened through the door to keep the cold from coming in. Melvin jumped up to greet her, as always. "Happy Sunday, Miss Teagan! And Happy New Year, too!"

"Hi, Melvin; same to you on both counts!" she replied as he walked with her through the lobby. Teagan nodded at Charlotte who was behind the desk; she was glad to see her scheduled and hoped to grab a few minutes of her time again.

She patted Melvin on the shoulder as Charlotte looked up and waved. "You should put this guy on the payroll. He could work in marketing – he's always at the door to greet people!"

"Well, not always," Charlotte said with a smile. "Any time you're in the building he's usually in the activity room. And hey, this morning, he wasn't there to greet me when I walked in at 10:00."

Teagan turned toward Melvin and lovingly scolded him. "Melvin, you're slipping! Why weren't you there to greet Miss Charlotte?"

Melvin's eyes twinkled. "That's because I was in the chapel this morning."

Teagan furrowed her brow. "But they had church yesterday, didn't they?"

"I wasn't there for church. I was watching the dancing girl."

This time both Teagan and Charlotte stopped and looked right at him.

"The dancing girl?" Charlotte inquired.

"Yup, the dancing girl." Melvin said, nodding his head.

"Melvin, there was a dancing girl – in the chapel?" Teagan had never remembered Melvin to be forgetful or out of touch, so this whole report was surprising.

"Yeah, she was there. She dances really good. I watched her the last time, too. Oh, gotta go," Melvin said as he spotted someone else coming in the door.

Teagan and Charlottelooked at each other and shrugged.

"That was kind of weird," Teagan said, watching him greet the lady who had just come in.

Charlotte nodded. "I'll have to check that out. I have no idea what he's talking about. And that's not like Melvin at all."

"Well, keep me posted," Teagan said. "And I may want to grab your ear later for a few minutes. Need a little more advice on that friend I had told you about last time."

Charlotte was on her way around the desk and gave Teagan a squeeze. "Any time is fine. But for now, you'd better down to activities. Your subjects will be protesting soon. Do we still have the author coming in this afternoon to read poetry?"

Teagan nodded. "Yup. I'll keep them busy for an hour or so and then give them a short break before rounding them up and heading to the library. Catch you later on."

She headed down to the activity room where a lot of her "regulars" were already waiting. Melvin had managed to sneak down ahead of her, and was sitting at his regular spot for bingo. "Good afternoon, everyone! So glad so many of you are here!"

Gladys rolled her eyes. "And where else would we be on Sunday? Now get this closet open so I can hand out the cards." Teagan saw the twinkle in her eye and knew there was no true urgency like her voice indicated, but she went right over to unlock the door for her. Gladys immediately grabbed the pile of cards and got to work, humming as she went.

"Now, remember gang," Teagan called out, "we're only playing for an hour today." Her announcement was met with groans until her added, "Remember, we have Scott Davies coming at 3:00 to read poetry from his new book. I hope a bunch of you will come to the library to hear him." She had read some of the the poems to the group earlier and they had loved his humor and wit about growing older, so she was thrilled when he agreed to come in person.

As she called numbers throughout the game, she noticed Ida arriving later and heading for the table with the crossword puzzle books. Teagan had just put a couple of new ones out, and she smiled when she saw Ida discovering them. The older woman glanced over at Teagan and mouthed the words "thank you" with a smile. Teagan nodded and winked, and Ida was lost in the puzzles as bingo finished up.

Melvin put the balls aways as Gladys collected the cards, so once again Teagan just had to collect all the bingo chip markers. As soon as he was finished, Melvin turned to go. "Gotta go sit at the door. I wanna greet the poet man!" Teagan laughed as he headed down the hall, wondering once again what the "dancing girl" in the chapel was all about.

She was glad that bingo had ended early as it gave her more time to visit with Ida. "I'm glad you found the new books," Teagan said warmly as she grabbed a chair.

Ida closed the one she was working on and smiled. "You take good care of me," she said, and then spotted Teagan's pin on her shirt and smiled. "You have it on."

Teagan's fingers went up to the pin she'd worn several times since receiving it. "That's because I love it," she said, "and so does everyone else who's seen it….well, except for maybe one person who I just don't get along with. I AM trying, but she sure makes it difficult."

Ida chuckled. "Ah, yes. People. Some can be wonderful, and others a challenge. And we just have to accept them wherever they are."

Teagan sensed that Ida was lost in a thought, and she seemed a bit sad as spoke. "Are you having trouble with someone here, Ida?"

"Oh, no, not at all. Everyone here has been wonderful." She patted Teagan's hand and gave her a weak smile. "No, I was referring to my Cassandra. I found out something that's troubling me, and I don't know what to do about it."

Now it was Teagan's turn to grasp the older woman's hands. "Your grand-daughter? She's not sick or anything?"

Ida shook her head. "No, it's nothing physical, my dear. I'm just not sure that Cassandra cares about me as much anymore – or maybe she's just going through some teenage angst – but I found out this morning that she's been lying to me, and I don't know whether I should tell Eliana about it or try to find out why first."

"Lying sounds kind of serious. I imagine that must make you sad." Teagan could see that Ida was torn. "And maybe you don't want to get her in trouble?"

Ida nodded as she looked up. "I can get over a grand-daughter not caring like she used to, but if she's lying about her whereabouts then I'm concerned for her safety. But I don't want to get her in trouble if it's nothing. Do you see my dilemma?"

"Cassandra is lucky to have a grandmother who cares so much – even if she doesn't see it right now. Maybe you can talk to her about it first before going to her mom. That way if it's nothing major she'll know that you trust her and maybe open up. And if it's something more, then you've given her a chance to explain herself before talking to Eliana. I don't know the details, but I guess if it was me, I'd want a chance to explain before being ratted out."

Ida's eyes were a bit misty, but she blinked back tears and nodded, patting Ida's hands. "Like your little owl friend," she said, glancing at the pin, "you are indeed wise beyond your years. I think I'll indeed wait until she comes to visit again, and then we can have a little talk. I hope." She straightened up, looked directly at Teagan, and added,

"Now tell me something totally different to take my mind off all of this."

Teagan loved how Ida just met her problems head on, and never let them get her down for long. "As a matter of fact, I have a question about food for you."

"You have me intrigued already."

"Well, my friend Brian is doing this project for his geography class where he's bringing in baked goods from all these different countries that they are studying."

"Sounds delicious."

Teagan nodded. "Believe me, it is. I've tried every item so far and they are all amazing. Which leads me to one of his upcoming areas in southern Europe. He was thinking of making something special from Greece, and I told him I knew just the person to ask. Was there a favorite dessert that you remember from growing up on Crete?"

Ida sat back and nodded. "Without a doubt. That would be louk-oumades."

"Sounds Greek to me," Teagan said laughing. "You'll have to tell me what that is."

"Loukomades are little Greek donuts that are fried and then drizzled with honey and walnuts. Oh, I'll never forget how delicate and sweet they were. There was a little market in Zaros run by an older gentleman and his wife. I think her loukoumades were even better than my grandmother's."

"Zaros? Is that where you lived?"

Ida nodded. "It's a little village on the south side of the island, right at the foothills of the mountains. You could see Mt. Ida from my back yard. There were olive trees all over – we used to call olive oil 'liquid gold' because it was such an important resource. That along with sultanas and spring water. All were abundant in Zaros."

"Sultanas? What are those?" Teagan asked.

"Those are the golden colored raisins that you can buy. Kissed and shriveled by the sun, my grandfather used to say."

Teagan glanced up at the clock, and hated that it was time to end this conversation. She loved Ida as if she were her own grandmother, but she also knew that she had a poet arriving shortly. Ida caught her glance and also looked at the clock.

"I've kept you from your work again, haven't I?" she said with a smile.

"Not a bit," Teagan replied. "Part of my job is to spend time with residents chatting, and you just happen to be the one I like chatting with the most." Ida smiled as she added, "Now, are you heading down to the library? I'd be happy to give you a push."

"I've love that," Ida replied, and they headed down the hall to find Melvin just greeting the author as he walked in. Teagan greeted him and led him to the library, where many residents waited already. After her introduction the residents clapped loudly and paid close attention as he began to read.

As she moved Ida up a bit closer, the older woman shivered a bit. "Chilly?" Teagan asked.

Ida nodded. "I should have brought my shawl. It always starts to get a litle cold later in the day." She glanced around looking to see if Charlotte or one of the aides was in sight. Seeing none, she turned to Teagan. "Maybe you could ask one of them to go and grab my shawl for me?"

"No need for that," Teagan replied. "I'd be happy to go and grab it for you. Although come to think of it, I've never been in your room, so I might need directions."

Ida chuckled. "Room 14 – down on your right. You'll see my shawl – the pretty one you gave me – hanging on the end of my bookshelf."

Teagan straightened up and whispered. "Back in a flash, my dear. Let me know if I miss anything."

She walked down the hall quickly and found Ida's room without any trouble. Ida had brought several pieces of her favorite furniture with her, and the room had a warm and cozy feel to it. She spotted the shawl she'd given her right where Ida said it would be, and she walked over to grab it for her. On top of her bookshelf were several photos, the first of which must have been a photo taken in Crete. Ida was a young girl standing beside an olive tree, a mountain in the background behind her. Teagan smiled. *"Ida in her backyard, just as she described,"* she thought.

The middle photo must have been her wedding picture, and Teagan was struck by how much Ida at a younger age looked like her daughter Eliana. She was a lovely bride. Teagan wondered what it must have been like to get married, despite having no desire for the marital relations that lay ahead.

Her eyes moved to the last photo, which was a picture of Ida with her family. As Teagan looked more closely, she gasped, bringing her hand up to her mouth. "Oh, my God! It can't be!" Staring back at her from the photo was Ida's grand-daughter. Her Cassandra. And Teagan's Cassie.

She stood there, all the different pieces of the puzzle swirling around her as they locked into place. Cassie. Running through the cemetery and turning toward Caldwell Manor. She wasn't running home – she was going to see her grandmother. Cassie. The one who was growing distant and didn't want to talk. Cassie. The one who was lying to her grandmother about her whereabouts. *"The dancing girl in the chapel,"* she thought. *"That has to be who Melvin saw."* Cassie.

Teagan's head was spinning, and she knew she had to get back to Ida with her shawl. *"But what will I say?"* she thought, standing there and staring at the photo. *"I just figured out that your beloved grand-daughter is the one I've had so much trouble with? The one who isn't anything like the girl you describe?"*

She slowly made her way back down the hall, not quite sure how to proceed. She approached Ida from the back, and she slowly wrapped the shawl around her shoulders as she tried to find words. "Here you are, Ida. This should help."

Ida reached up and squeezed her hand, and then looked up to see Teagan's face. Her expression immediately turned to concern. "Honey, what's the matter? You look like you just saw a ghost."

Teagan felt like she had. "I just found something out that's a bit troubling, that's all. I'll be fine once I have time to process it. I'll be back in a few minutes."

With that she headed to the activity room, which she prayed

would be empty – and it was. She slumped into a chair and put her head on her arms, trying to blot out the image of Cassie in the photo. Her Cassandra. The girl who all of sudden had two faces, and she didn't know which was which.

She heard a noise behind her, and turned to see Maggie wheeling Ida up to the table. "Thank you, Maggie," the older woman said as the social worker took a step back and looked at Teagan.

"Hope it's okay. She grabbed my arm as I walked by and insisted that we follow you."

"It's fine, Maggie. Thanks." The social worker nodded and walked back out of the room. Ida turn to Teagan and placed her hand on her arm. "Now do you want to tell me what's really going on?"

Teagan's eyes welled up. How could this wonderful woman be Cassie's grandmother? And how would everything change now?

"Ida," she murmured, her lips trembling. "It's just that I found something out….in your room….the photo…."

"The photo? Which photo, dear?"

"The one with Cassandra." Teagan looked directly at this woman who had become so special to her. "Your Cassandra is the girl I've had so much trouble with. She goes by Cassie at school – it never occurred to me that it was a nickname. But how could she be the same girl?"

She let the tears come, and Ida stroked her arm lovingly to help her calm down.

When finally Teagan was quiet, Ida folded her hands on the table in front of her. "Well," she began, "This certainly gives us both something to think about, doesn't it? It seems you already know my Cassan —Cassie pretty well. And you've apparently seen another side of her than the girl I know – or did know. She's slowly become someone else, or is at least dealing with something that she doesn't want to talk about."

Teagan swallowed hard. "I hope I'm wrong, but I think I know exactly what she's dealing with. I've seen it before, but didn't understand it back then."

"What do you mean?"

"I think she's suffering from anorexia, or maybe another eating disorder. And I'm scared. for her."

Ida looked pensive, but leaned in forward. "Tell me everything you know, dear."

Teagan shared all of the interactions she'd had with Cassie so far. The running in the cemetery, the playing with food, the fear about fat people, and even the dancing girl in the chapel. "I don't know if that was really her, but Melvin said she was really good, and it was a Sunday morning. You said she'd been in to see you."

Ida nodded. "So that's where she goes. She tells her mother she's coming to visit, and then disappears to go and dance after a few minutes."

It was Teagan's turn to hold her friend's hand. "I suspect that's when she was in the cemetery as well. She probably went jogging before the weather got cold."

Ida nodded. "I believe you're right. Which means Cassandra's been both lying about her whereabouts to her mother AND sneaking off to exercise. Put that together with your anecdotes from the mall and I think we indeed have an issue we'll have to deal with. Maybe I should call Eliana and have her come over…"

Teagan shook her head. "We have to go about it the right way or she'll get even more defensive and harder to reach. I wish we'd hit if off better – aside from rehearsal I just don't know how I'd even have the chance to try and talk to her."

Ida clasped her arm. "Wait! Are you saying that Cassandra is in the show with you? She hasn't said anything to me."

Teagan hesitated. "She actually has the other female lead, and she's amazing on stage – especially her dancing."

"A lead?" Teagan couldn't tell if she looked more hurt or proud. "There was a time when she would have called to tell me right away…..and now – not even Eliana has told me about it."

"I suspect Cassie – Cassandra – maybe asked her not to? I know from what I've read that many times people with anorexia don't want to call attention to themselves. Especially if it's something to be proud of."

Ida took Teagan's hand again. "I know you've been through this before. That has to make it even harder to want anything to do with Cassandra. And you can call her Cassie – it's how you know her."

Teagan smiled weakly. "It's okay. I admit I haven't hit it off with her from the start, but as I started to note things I realized that I might be the only one seeing the clues—"

"Because of Joanne?"

Teagan nodded. And no matter how I feel about her, I don't want to lose another person to this disease. Not if there's anything I can do to help."

Ida squeezed her hands and nodded. "Well, then, my dear, we are a team. From here on, our number one goal is to try and get my granddaughter the help that she desperately needs. Do we have a deal?"

Teagan nodded back. "Absolutely. Let's do this. Let's try to reach her. Together."

CHAPTER 18

Rehearsal the next day was going to involve blocking for two very physical scenes between Teagan and Mike. At one point he was supposed to pick her up and carry her offstage over his shoulder as she pounded his back. Teagan already knew that changes would need to be made, and she hoped she wouldn't be judged for it.

As she headed down the hall to the auditorium, a movement caught her eye as she passed the chorus room across the hall. She peeked through the window, and sighed. Cassie was dancing alone, going over choreography routines – again and again. Teagan wanted to go in and start a conversation, if only to stop the physical activity that had become an obsession. She glanced at her watch and knew it would have to wait. She had to be on stage in five minutes, so she continued on and headed in to rehearsal. She and Mike would be blocked first, and then others would join them for the final scene of the first act.

They had already had a couple of physical scenes as Petruchio and Kate, and Teagan loved the chemistry between them for the bantering scenes. This one would be a more intense, and while she was ready for the challenge, she wondered about the ending.

As Mr. C walked them through the scene, Teagan found herself getting lost in the character of Kate again. First she and Petruchio argued about her marrying him, and then the fight became physical as he demanded that she kiss him. As she and Mike threw barbs across the table, she felt him grab her wrist. She screamed and tried to kick him, only to have him now hold both her wrist and ankle. Her dress would no doubt fall down here and show off her pantaloons underneath, and Teagan continued trying to kick Mike in character until he had her on top of the table and he was straddled across her, holding her arms down. Mike was breathing heavy, as was Teagan. She wasn't used to such close physical contact, and she was really self conscious of Mike being on top of her. Teagan raised her head and screamed as loud as she could, spitting out several insults in his face. At this point Baptista, her father in the show, walked in and found them in a compromising position, and the match was agreed upon for the marriage.

In response, Teagan continued on as Kate, trying to kick her partner every chance she got. When Petruchio got fed up enough, he grabbed her, sat down, and pulled her over his lap, giving her rear a couple of slaps to end the scene before the wedding. Teagan heard Mike grunt a bit when she landed on his lap, and hoped that she didn't hurt anything. It was the second time she felt self-conscious of her size.

"Cut!" interjected Mr. C. Teagan was suddenly more aware that she and Mike had an audience. The ensemble members had been filing in for rehearsal, and they were now all seated in the audience watching the big fight scene. All of them erupted in claps and whistles as Mike gave Teagan a hand and helped her off the table. Her face was as flushed as his.

Mr. C. was beaming. "That scene was fabulous! You guys will bring the house down with that fight. Now take five and rest a few and we'll bring the ensemble up to do the wedding scene."

Teagan sighed heavily as she reached for a water bottle. "Sorry if I was heavier than you're used to having on your lap," she said sheepishly to Mike.

He grinned. "Don't worry about it. Man, you were on fire, girl – I was almost scared of ya."

Teagan swallowed some cold water and remained silent, not quite knowing how to respond. She finally turned to him and said, "Thanks. I'm thinking we may need to talk to Mr. C about the end of the next scene. I don't think it will work for you to pick me up and sling me over your shoulder."

Mike eyed her up and down, no doubt trying to assess whether he could handle it. "You might be right. Maybe I can just wrap my arms around you and drag you off backwards instead. I wouldn't wanna drop you. Although it might be fun to give it a shot."

Teagan was confused. *"God, is he hitting on me again?"* she thought. She wished she had a better radar for knowing. Either way, he wouldn't get anywhere. She scanned the audience to see if Cassie had come to watch the scene. She was sitting with Julia and Kyleigh on one side, but just when she had come in Teagan didn't know. She hoped to find some way to have a conversation – preferably not one where they were yelling at each other.

As the wedding scene was blocked, Teagan found herself apprehensive about the ending. Mike would try to kiss her at the end of the song, and she got to slap him as Kate. That she knew she could do, although she was a little worried about hurting him. But that's when he would pick her up, and she didn't know whether Mr. C would expect it as written or stop them with other directions.

When the slap came, Teagan tried not to use full force, but she could see Mike's eyes widen when her hand hit his cheek. He grabbed her wrist and spun her around, wrapping his arms around her waist while holding her wrists. As the scene ended, he pulled her backwards in this position, with her fighting to get free and protesting along the way. Mr. C had trusted them to try something on their own, and from his reaction they'd made a good choice.

"Okay, everyone, listen up!" Mr. C shouted over the cast as they broke into conversation. "That's it for full cast – you worked hard today, and you're free to go. We've got just about all the big scenes done, and we'll be picking up the pace in terms of starting to put this all together. See you all tomorrow ready to go through the big numbers of the second act. After that we start running the show from the beginning. Great job, today!"

As others began heading down the stairs, Mr. C addressed both Teagan and Mike. "I liked your choice today. I decided to see what your characters would do before I changed the blocking, but I like where you went on your own. We'll leave that in." He looked down at his notes, and then continued, "The only other thing we haven't finished blocking is the final scene, with the last song and major kiss. We'll be doing that tomorrow, so if you two need to get it out of your system, you can stay and practice once or twice before kissing in front of the whole cast." He turned his attention elsewhere and started walking away. "I gotta meet with the lighting designer. See you tomorrow."

Suddenly Teagan felt extremely self-conscious. Even though there was no attraction, she still felt apprehensive about her first kiss. She had no idea what to expect or whether she even knew what to do.

Mike had sat on the side of the table, one foot still on the floor. He smirked a bit and said, "So, we're supposed to practice kissin', are we? I think I might enjoy that."

Teagan looked at him and raised her eyebrows. "Enjoy it?"

He flashed her a smile. "Not gonna lie, Teagan. Those scenes today? I was a little turned on by all that sass comin' out of you. Especially those fight scenes when we were a little more up close and personal."

Now Teagan was sure he was hitting on her, and her first response was anger. "Aren't you supposed to dating Cassie?" She fired at him. "Somehow I don't think it's entirely proper to be dating one girl and hitting on another." She folded her arms across her chest and ended with "Correct me if I'm wrong."

Mike held his hands up as he tried to explain. "Whoa! Lighten up. Look, I really DO like Cassie, and we've had some fun hangin' out. But I'm just not sure about her, you know? I mean, I really like her, but she's so damn insecure and fragile sometimes. And she always wants to control every minute we're together."

He ran his hand through his hair and shook his head, then looked up at Teagan. "Look, I've just never met anyone like you. You're so direct and sure of yourself , and you don't play any of the games that other girls play. It's damn refreshing – even if you're not at all the type I'm usually attracted to."

Teagan chuckled as she took a few steps toward him. "You mean fat?"

Mike nodded. "Like *that*. I mean, you just come out and say that you're fat, and it doesn't seem to bother you at all. Every other girl I've dated is all bent out of shape about her size, and thinks she's fat even when she's not. What's with you? What makes you so damn confident?"

Teagan felt more powerful and sure of herself as the conversation continued. She moved next to Mike and leaned against the table beside him. "I hate living in a world where your size defines you. I'm like every other girl – I just happen to be in a fat body. I still talk and think and move around like everyone else….I just have more of it, that's all."

"Well, it's mind-blowing. And really attractive."

Teagan took a deep breath. "Well, I'm about to blow your mind a second time then. It's time to tell you something else about me. One that's a little more relevant to this kissing scene."

Mike sat up straighter and turned toward her more. "Tell me more, kiddo. I'm all ears."

Teagan laughed nervously. "I wouldn't waste your energy getting all excited about it. It's not you, Mike, it's just –"

"You're dating that Brian guy, aren't you?"

"Brian? Oh, God, no! I'm not interested in anyone right now– or ever. I'm what they call asexual and aromantic, or ace/aro. No physical or romantic attraction. It's just not there. Never has been. Never will be. Not for me."

Mike tilted his head sideway a bit and grinned. "Or maybe….you haven't met the right person yet to turn you on?" His hand reached over to take a hold of Teagan's hand.

Teagan pulled it back and groaned. "That's such a normal response

– and so wrong. It's not a phase, or a case of not finding my Prince Charming. It's a part of who I am. And I'm totally content with it. Just like my fat doesn't define me? Neither does my sexuality. I hope you can get that."

Mike rubbed his mouth with his hand. "A little weird, not gonna lie. Hey, I'm a guy. It's a lot weird, actually."

This made Teagan laugh, and both relaxed a bit.

"So," Mike continued, "just how does this work with the whole kiss thing? What should I expect? You're not gonna whack me or anything, are you?"

Teagan stood up and faced him, knowing the time had come to get it over with. "Actually, Mike, this will be my very first kiss, so you'll have to wait and see. And I'm trusting that you'll walk me through it, 'cause I really don't have a clue."

Mike reached out his hand, and this time she took it, stepping in closer to him.

"I'm a pretty good teacher, I think," Mike said as he cupped her face with his hands. "Let's get this lesson started, shall we?" Teagan closed her eyes, because she'd seen enough movies to know that was normal behavior, and Mike's lips were warm on hers. He pulled her closer as lips pressed harder, and then he slowly pulled away, his breath still warm on her face.

"How'd I do?" she murmured.

"Kinda like when I bluff my way through an essay and still get an A. That was a mighty fine kiss, kiddo."

Teagan stepped back, wiping her mouth off with the back of hand. "I guess I'm glad we did get that out of the way before tomorrow. Might have been super awkward."

"Trust me," Mike said, "it'll still be awkward."

"I hope Cassie's okay with it," Teagan began, "I really don't need anything more to fuel the fire."

"Yeah, what's with you two? You hardly seem to know each other, but she seems so intimidated by you. And kinda nasty at times."

"I think I actually know her better than most right now. And I think most of the hostility toward me right now is fear."

"Fear? What the hell's she afraid of? You?"

"Actually, yeah. I'm sure that Cassie has a huge problem. And I think she suspects that I know, and that scares the hell out of her."

Mike looked concerned. "What problem? Is she sick or something?"

Teagan nodded. "Yeah, she is. I'm positive she has an eating disorder. Anorexia. And I really need to find a way to get her help – I promised a friend I would."

Mike sat quietly for a minute, then looked up at Teagan. "I think you're right. Whenever we've been out, I've never seen her eat – even if there's food in front of her. And she's always really cold and wears a ton of layers – almost like she's trying to hide."

"She probably is. In her mind she thinks she's fat. Anorexia distorts the body image. While I'm content with my size, Cassie will never be. No matter how thin she gets, she'll always see herself as fat. And she'll try to control that in ways that are super unhealthy."

"So what can we do?" Mike asked. "I'm in. I'll help any way I can. Just tell me what to do."

"I will," Teagan replied with a smile. "As soon as I have it figured out myself."

CHAPTER 19

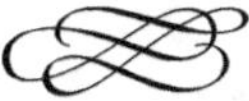

$\mathcal{A}$ few nights later Teagan and Brian headed to Gino's for dinner.

"I swear I never get to see you anymore, girl," Brian said as they walked in and waved at Gino behind the counter. "Except at rehearsals, when we never get to talk."

Gino stepped around to greet them.

"My two favorite young people! It's been too long! Are you just picking up and leaving again, or are you finally going to let Gino get you that romantic little table tonight, eh?" He opened his arms wide and smiled from ear to ear. "It's almost Valentine's Days, after all...."

Brian grinned. "Okay, Gino, you win." He winked at Teagan and then continued, "we'll take the most romantic table you've got. Nothing's too special for my girl here." He wrapped his arm around her and squeezed, and Teagan had to bite her lip not to burst out laughing.

Gino grabbed two menus and gestured with his arm to follow. "You come with me. You know Gino will take extra special care of you tonight!" He sat them down at a cozy table in the corner and hummed as he walked away.

"Your girl, huh?" Teagan asked, giggling.

"Hey, I made his day. And what the heck? Sometimes it's just easier to play along than explain it all. Am I right?"

"That's for sure. I know I tried to explain it to Mike at rehearsal one day, but I'm pretty sure he thinks his kiss was gonna help make me normal."

"Not gonna lie. It looked pretty convincing when you two kissed in that last scene." Brian opened his menu and winked at her. "I almost got a little jealous."

Teagan laughed. "Honey, if I was going to go after any guy, you would have been it a long time ago. But hey, how are things in that department?"

Brian flashed a smile that told her all she needed to know.

"Lou and I have been talking a lot more. And yesterday he sort of asked me out for Valentine's Day."

Teagan squealed, clapping her hands over her mouth to quiet herself down.

"That's awesome! So.....where are you going? Romantic dinner?" She leaned in with a smirk on her face. "Should I have Gino save this table for that night?"

"No way – it might kill him! Besides, it's nothing that romantic. We're going bowling. Should be fun."

"I really AM happy for you – you know that, right?"

"Yeah, I do, Teags. And I'm glad that my best friend isn't the jealous type."

With that, he turned his attention to the menu. "So what are gonna have? We should probably decide before Gino gets back or he'll have us eating oysters."

Teagan laughed out loud. "You better decide quick, 'cause he's on his way."

Later on, as Brian swirled his pasta around his eggplant parmagiana and Teagan took another bite of her calzone, she filled him in on Cassie being Ida's granddaughter, as well as the talk she'd had with Mike about Cassie's eating disorder.

"Wow," Brian said, "You've had a crap load to deal with, haven't you?"

"It's been rough, not gonna lie. I still can't believe she's the same girl that Ida has told me about all these months. For instance, remember that time in the seventh grade when we bought Joanne tickets for her birthday to see Fiddler?"

Brian took a swig of water. "That was an awesome show. And God, she was happy that night. She sang those songs for weeks."

She nodded. "It turns out Cassie was up visiting Ida that year, and they were at the same show. Turns out Fiddler is HER favorite show, too."

"Wow," Brian said, his fork midway to his mouth. "It's almost weird how much Cassie and Joanne have in common. Theater, dance......anorexia...."

Teagan nodded, but she realized she wasn't tearing up anymore when she talked about Joanne's illness. Instead, she had a firm resolve to make sure Cassie didn't follow down that path.

"I talked to Charlotte, the nurse at work, and then she had me talk to one of the social workers – her name's Maggie – and it turns out that she struggled with anorexia when she was our age. She suggested that Ida has her family over to Caldwell Manor for a visit. Charlotte and Maggie will be there, too. We're going to have an intervention or sorts, and see if we can convince her to go inpatient for treatment. There's a really good facility over on the other side of Brentwood, and Charlotte said she thinks there are open beds."

"But what about the show? She's got a major lead."

"There's only a couple more weeks until the show's over, so we'll wait until after. Just knowing we have a plan helps."

Brian shook his head. "A couple of weeks. Man, this year's just flying by, isn't it? It seems like just yesterday I was screaming at you that you'd gotten the role of Kate."

"Overall, it's been a really good year. There's a lot going on, but I'm really glad I did it. Not just to keep the promise to Joanne, but because I think it's been a good year for me to find myself and be more sure of who I am."

"And you think Joanne didn't know all that when she made you promise? She knew you so damn well, Teags. And she knew that you needed to make some new friends. You know, ones that aren't in their eighties."

Teagan almost spilled her drink as she remembered something. "That reminds me! I have another baking request for you. It's really important!"

"I'm all ears."

"Okay, so next week is Ida's birthday, and she's insisting that I come for a little dinner celebration. Her family is gonna be there, so maybe I can actually try to make a little headway with Cassie. But Ida was telling me about her childhood on Crete, and there's a special dessert she remembers having that I'd love to surprise her with. Think you can handle it?"

"A baking challenge?" he asked with a grin. "Lay it on me – you know I'm in!"

"They're called loukoumades. Ida described them as little Greek donuts with drizzled honey and walnuts on top. I'd really like to bring those instead of a cake. I'll have her tell Eliana that I'm bringing the cake as my gift. I think she'll be really surprised."

"Well, technically, I'M bringing the cake. Is that really your gift, or are getting her something else?"

Teagan smiled. "I found the perfect book online. It's a picture history of Crete. Has tons of photos, and I'm sure it will bring back lots of memories for her. I'm excited to give it to her. But she'll love the loukoumades more, I guarantee it."

"Tell you what – just to make sure they're warm, let me know the date and time and I'll deliver them myself – how's that for service?"

"You're awesome. And I know Ida will love meeting my best friend."

CHAPTER 20

The day of Ida's birthday party was also the day of Teagan's presentation with Barb in health class. She had enjoyed working with Barb, and felt that their project really got through to the class. There were lots of questions at the end, and they fielded them thoroughly. By the end of class, many peers were stopping by to pick up a handout with resource numbers. Teagan gratefully fingered her owl pin, which she'd worn for good luck.

She was also realizing that she might need luck that night. While she and Cassie had managed to develop a civil relationship on stage, she knew that there was still a wall between them. If Teagan was going to be able to confront Cassie about her anorexia, she felt that she still needed to find more common ground between them. She hoped that the evening at Caldwell Manor would help toward that goal. She also wondered if Cassie would even make it. She had missed other major holidays claiming to be sick. Teagan prayed that she would be there for Ida's birthday. She still didn't know that Teagan worked there and was so close to her grandmother, so tonight would be a big surprise on her part. Ida had assured her that all would be fine, and was so excited to finally bring her two favorite young people together face to face. *"Let's hope you're right, Ida,"* Teagan thought as she headed out to the bus.

Ida had requested that a little table be set up in the library for her birthday celebration. Many of the other residents did the same for special occasions, and the staff had done a beautiful job in setting up a lovely table. They hung a big "Happy Birthday" banner on the wall, and had white twinking lights along the book shelves for added atmosphere.

Teagan waited in the dining room until she saw the family arrive, and let our a sigh of relief to see Cassie was with them. Ida had even managed to have Cassie sit on the chair next to her. Once they were all settled, it was time to make an entrance. She carried a portable stereo and a CD into the room, and warmly greeted Ida's family.

She could see Cassie's jaw drop open as she entered the room. "It's so nice to see all of you. I'm so glad that you could be here to celebrate this special lady's birthday." Teagan plugged in the stereo and pushed a button, and soft Greek folk music filled the air. Ida clasped her hands together, her eyes twinkling.

"It's like being back home! Teagan, come…." She patted the seat on the other side of her, and Teagan slowly approached Ida and her grand-daughter.

"I guess you weren't exactly expecting to see me here, huh?"

Cassie shook her head, almost glaring but not quite.

Ida reached out and took each of their hands, looking from one to the other.

"Cassandra, I know that you already know Teagan. She's been such a good friend to me, and reminds me very much of you." Before Cassie could open her mouth to protest, she continued. "She also told me that you didn't exactly hit it off at first, but I know both of you, and I think you should give each other a chance. You might not hate her if you got to know like I do."

Ida patted Cassie's hand, and glanced over at Teagan with a smile.

"And now," she said, turning back to Cassie, "I want to hear all about this theater production. Rumor has it that you are quite the actress."

Teagan wasn't sure if Cassie would flip out that her involvement in the show was known, but Cassie answered quietly. "It's okay, I guess. The role is kinda fun. And I like the dancing."

"Your dancing is amazing," Teagan said as she looked directly at Cassie. "Every time you're on stage everyone is just mesmerized." She turned to Ida and added,"You should come to see her. I know how much you loved being at the theater with her growing up."

Cassie looked puzzled. Teagan smiled. "Do you remember when your grandmother took you to the Brentwood Playhouse for Fiddler on the Roof?" She saw a flicker of genuine caring and connection between Cassie and Ida as the memory materialized. "I was actually there the same night? Weird, huh?"

"Really? That was, like, seventh grade."

Ida smiled. "Cassandra, dear, Teagan has lived in Caldwell all her life. And she's loved theater just like you have. She was there that night with her best friend, and we were probably only a few rows apart from each other. What a coincidence, don't you think?"

"I guess," Cassie answered, but her tone had softened. She turned to Teagan and asked, "so did your friend move away? 'Cause I usually see you hanging out with Brian."

Teagan took a deep breath, deciding not to reveal too much tonight. She didn't want to see walls that were slowly coming down fly back up in a moment's time. "No, my friend died. The following year."

Cassie sat quietly. "Sorry. Really. That must have been hard."

Teagan nodded. "Toughest thing in my life to go through. But it gets easier."

At that moment, staff announced that they were bringing dinner in, and Teagan gave silent thanks that the topic had been broached, but not discussed at length. That conversation would wait for another day. The family gathered around the table, and Teagan helped the staff to serve everyone.

Eliana had arranged to have a catered meal brought in with some of Ida's favorites, and Teagan noticed that Cassie seemed a bit more animated in conversation, even if there was so little on the plate in front of her. She had a normal serving of green beans, a small piece of fish, and a spoonful of rice. As she passed the serving bowls to her brother Philip, he at one point glanced over at her plate and shook his head.

"Sis, you eat like a bird," he said, as he heaped his plate with rice.

"All the more for you," Cassie retorted, as she rearranged the vegetables on her plate.

Teagan knew that for tonight, it was important to just keep Cassie engaged and let the food issue go. That confrontation would come soon enough.

"So, I know you dance at the studio now. How do like Miss Colleen?"

"She's pretty nice, but she can be a little tough some days."

Teagan grinned. "Does she still make you dance the waltz combination across the floor by yourself if you're not paying attention?

Cassie looked up and Teagan saw what looked like a little smile. "Yeah. I heard that you used to dance there, too."

"Joanne and I were in classes with Kyleigh and Julia. And Miss Colleen will tell ya that I did a lot of those combos across the floor. But she's about the best teacher around for technique."

Cassie nodded. "I've progressed way more since moving here than when I danced in Texas. So why did you quit?"

Teagan blinked for a minute. She'd never really thought of herself as a quitter. Yes, she had stepped back when she was doing therapy a couple of times a week, and then got a job that gave her a new focus. But she always thought she might go back someday.

"When Joanne died I just lost it for awhile, and wasn't capable of dancing – or doing anything, really, except therapy. I always told myself I'd go back, but then I started working here, and school got tougher, and now it's three years later and I know how rusty I am. Thankfully I don't have nearly the amount of dance moves that you do on stage. You really are one of the best dancers out there."

"I don't know. Julia and Kyleigh are both really good. And there's that freshman girl, too – I forget her name – but she's unreal for her age."

Teagan smiled. "That's Beth Newton, Joanne's little sister. I've watched her grow up since she was a baby. I'm so glad that she decided to try out as a freshman – it's been great being able to have her there."

Teagan noticed Ida had stopped eating and was just sitting there watching them with a contented smile on her face. "I think this is the best birthday I've ever had," she said softly, "and I'm so happy to have my two favorite young people on either side of me to share it with."

Teagan smiled at Ida, and then her eyes locked with Cassie's, who for once wasn't looking angry or scared. Cassie turned to the older woman and patted her hand.

"I'm glad you're having a good birthday, Gram. You deserve it more than anyone I know." Teagan knew that she was sincere, and for once could see the bond between them.

As she silently gave thanks, she noticed Brian heading in door with a big oval platter covered with a silver lid.

Eliana spotted him as well, and used her spoon to clink her water glass.

"Everyone, I believe that Teagan arranged to have the cake delivered for the birthday girl, and if I'm not mistaken, that's what just arrived with this young man?"

Teagan stood up and nodded, grinning at Brian who carefully made his way to the table. "This is one of my best friends, Brian Morris, who is also an incredible baker. I asked him if he could make something special for tonight."

Turning to Ida, she continued, "I hope you aren't too disappointed that I chose something other than cake. I totally trust Brian's abilities, but I guess you'll be the final judge." She raised her glass, and gestured for others to do the same. "Happy birthday, Ida!"

As everyone wished her well, Brian carefully removed the silver lid.

Ida clasped her hands in front as her eyes got wide and her smile got wider.

"Loukoumades!"

"Donuts?" blurted Philip. "You got DONUTS for your birthday?"

Ida beamed at her grandson. "These aren't just donuts, my dear. These are a special dessert that I used to eat when I was even younger than you and still lived on Crete." She smiled up at Brian and added, "and they look delectable!"

"Allow me to add the final touch," Brian said grinning. He reached into his pocket and pulled out a candle, stuck it into the middle of the plate, and addressed the family as he lit it. "Now SING – and make it pretty!"

Once everyone was served some loukoumades and vanilla ice cream, all conversation was put on hold as each enjoyed their desserts. Ida took one bite, closed her eyes, and sighed.

She opened her eyes and looked across to where Brian had pulled up a chair to join them. "Thank you. This has brought me back to places in my childhood that I'd forgotten. Memories that are full of love and happy times. And you," she said, turning to Teagan, "thank you for thinking of this. This was a perfect way to end the best birthday ever."

Eliana smiled from across the table. "Well, it might not be QUITE over yet, mother. I think there are still a couple of surprises. Philip, do you want to get the gifts?"

Philip jumped up and walked over to the corner, grabbing a tote bag. He returned to the table and pulled out a few gifts from inside and placed them in front of Ida. "Happy birthday, Grandma," he said quietly. Ida wrapped her arm around him and gave him a hug.

"Thank you, Philip," she said, leaning up to kiss him on the cheek. Teagan chuckled to herself as she watched him squirm away and wipe his mouth with his sleeve. She watched Ida open several gifts – one auburn sweater, some lavender scented lotion, and a package with three crossword puzzle books in it.

"That one's from me, Grandma," said Philip. "I know they're your favorite."

Ida looked at her grandson and smiled. "You're right, Philip. It helps to keep my brain sharp. I think even Teagan would approve. Usually she's the one giving me puzzle books."

With that, Teagan pulled a wrapped package out from her own bag and slid it across to her friend. "Not a puzzle book, but I hope it will still keep the brain chugging along."

When Ida unwrapped the book, she sat without speaking for a moment as she gazed at the cover of *The History of Crete in Photos.* She ran her fingers over some of the photos on the front of the cover and Teagan could see her eyes misting up a bit.

"Thank you, my dear," Ida whispered as she turned her gaze toward her. "This will be a special journey reading through this."

Philip broke up the sentimental moment. "Hey, sis, where's the one from you?"

Cassie looked insecure and doubtful as she removed a flat gift from her purse. "It's nothing special, Gram," she stammered. "I just remembered you had asked about it, so…" Her voice trailed off as Ida took the gift from her. She unwrapped the shiny blue paper to find a beautiful framed photo of Cassie at the dance studio. Teagan immediately recognized the back drop for the annual professional photos that were taken to coincide with Christmas gift giving.

Ida reached over and caressed the side of Cassie's face. "My dear Cassandra," she murmured, "nothing makes my heart sing more than seeing you perform. This will be cherished. Thank you."

Cassie swallowed hard and reached up to cover her grandmother's hand on her cheek. "I know I'm not here as much I could be, but I do love you, Gram."

Teagan was sure that more than the three of them had to blink tears away. She glanced over and caught Brian's expression, and as their eyes met she mouthed "thank you" to him and smiled. It had been a wonderful birthday celebration indeed.

CHAPTER 21

A week later, Teagan found herself in the middle of "tech" week, the week just before opening night where all of the technical aspects of the show had to be ironed out. Lighting, music, and sound cues were coordinated and written down. Stage crew members ran through the actual scene changes by moving various backdrops, pieces of furniture, and other items. Each new scene created was then "marked" as they put special tape on the floor around the corners of each set piece and labeled them with marker. The process was long, often boring, and totally necessary for the success of the production.

In addition to all of the technical aspects coming together, cast members performed the show each night in full costume and make-up, singing and dancing in front of hot, bright lights, all with no audience to give them any energy back. Almost every cast member was tired, but trying their best to give a strong performance.

When Teagan and Brian arrived at the school, they hugged for good luck and headed off to get into costume. This was the last official rehearsal; tomorrow the stage was "dark", in that they all finally had one night off to rest and get ready for the following night's opening. Teagan was exhausted, and so ready for a night off.

As she applied her make-up, she nodded to Paula who came in and sat down next to her. "You look tired, girl," Paula said as she took items out of her bag.

"Exhausted," Teagan replied. "I've had a blast, but I am SO looking forward to having some quiet time next week."

"Amen. I think all of us feel that way." Paula patted some foundation on her face, and as she used her fingers to evenly rub it over her cheeks, she made eye contact with Teagan in the mirror in front of them. "By the way, in case I don't get a chance to tell you, you've been phenomenal as Lilli. It's been great being able to work with you."

Teagan turned to face her. "I've made some good friends, and you're definitely one of them." She saw Paula grin, and then noticed Cassie across the room fixing her hair. "Hey, I wanna go say hi to Cassie – I'll catch you on stage."

Cassie smiled weakly as Teagan approached. She was tucking her real hair under a wig and fastening it. Teagan noted that Cassie looked more tired than ever, as dark circles peeked through the foundation under her eyes.

"Hey. Just wanted to come over and wish you good luck tonight. It's been a tough few nights, and tonight will be the worst. I feel like I could lay down and sleep for a week."

"I hear ya…I am so tired. At least we have tomorrow night off."

Teagan added, "And we'll have the audience the next night. That will give us some energy back."

They both sat quietly for a moment, and then Cassie turned to Teagan and looked straight at her. "Look, I know we haven't exactly gotten along so far. But the other night at Gram's party…" she paused for a moment. "I think I misjudged you. And I know how much you care about my Gram, and that means a lot."

Teagan found herself getting emotional. "I misjudged you, too. I thought you were kind of snotty. But now I know you've just been dealing with major changes in your life, like moving up from Texas. No one knows how hard it is to have your world turned upside down better than me."

At that moment Ann Kirkland, the stage manager, popped her

head in the door and yelled, "Five minutes!" This was the signal that all actors needed to be in place within five minutes.

As she got up to leave, Teagan placed her hand on Cassie's shoulder and looked at her in the mirror. "Maybe when the show is over....we can hang out a little. Something to think about."

"Maybe. That might be nice."

Teagan took a deep breath and straightened up. "Well," she said, breaking the tension, "break a leg!" She headed out into the hallway where Beth Newton almost ran into her.

"Teagan!" Beth cried. "I'm *so* glad I saw you! I wanted to wish you *tons* of luck tonight. You're so amazing!" And as she excitedly skipped away, she turned back and called out, "and my sister is so proud of you!"

Teagan blew her a kiss and stepped backstage. Brian was already in place, and gave her a quick hug as she passed by. "Go get 'em, Teags." She hugged him back, and took her spot backstage next to Paula.

"One more time and we get a night off," Paula whispered.

"Music to my ears. Let's do this!"

As the overture began, Teagan found new energy. While she was still tired, the characters that she played were not, and she got her strength from them. The opening scenes went well, and she managed to sing the first romantic song with Mike without too much awkwardness. When she changed into her costume for the role of Kate, she found herself chuckling. *"Here I am backstage,"* she thought, *"practically ripping the clothes off my big sweaty body to change into a much more revealing outfit, and I could care less who walks by and sees. I love theater!"*

She heard the music for Cassie's big song and dance number with her three suitors, and quietly moved to a spot offstage where she could watch from the side. Cassie's voice seemed tired, and Teagan was concerned about how the long rehearsals were affecting the actress under the bright lights. She was still amazed at how well Cassie danced, despite her worries about how much nutrition she was actually taking in. *"Just a few more nights,"* Teagan thought, *"and then we need to sit down and really talk about what's going on."* She shivered a bit just thinking about how difficult it would be, but hoped that they were catching Cassie's disease earlier on.

Teagan watched as Cassie danced on top of a table, spinning about and then jumping into the arms of the three male dancers. Teagan caught her breath when she saw Cassie falter slightly on her landing, holding on to one of the other dancers for a split second longer than normal. Luckily there was just one more spin and the song came to an end. As Cassie came offstage Teagan was waiting for her.

"Are you okay?" she asked, grasping Cassie's arms.

"I'm fine," Cassie stammered. "Just a little dizzy from the spinning, that's all. Go on, your cue's coming up." She nodded her head in the direction of Teagan's entrance. "I'll be out there soon enough."

Teagan smiled weakly. "Okay," she whispered, giving Cassie's arms a squeeze.

Teagan loved this scene. Since last week's dinner at Caldwell Manor, she and Cassie had really clicked on stage as sisters Kate and Bianca. There was a new trust between them, and their fight scene was stronger because of it. She was excited to have Ida see the two of them in this scene, as it was the best acting that each actress did in a scene together.

As a warm up she did some screaming and threw a few things at a few of the suitors that had just danced with Bianca. As Cassie entered as Bianca, Teagan turned toward her. Their dialogue was quick and witty, with verbals barbs and physical gestures of envy. Kate knew that Bianca was the preferred daughter and she was direct in showing it. Bianca knew that she'd never be free to marry if Kate didn't find a husband first, and she both hated her and pleaded with her to change her ways.

As the scene grew, so did their intensity. When Bianca finally came to try and grab hold of Kate, Teagan turned to her and raised her broom, ready to strike. In a split second, her heart sank. She saw Cassie's eyes start to roll back, and felt her grip on her dress release as she started to slump to the floor.

"*Cassie!*" Teagan screamed, dropping the broom and managing to catch Cassie before she hit her head. She lowered the actress to the floor as cast members came from everywhere.

"Oh my God!" Paula cried out, "Get some help!"

Teagan held her breath as she checked for Cassie's pulse and found it without any trouble. As cast members crowded around, she spoke sternly. "Everyone back up – she's just fainted."

"That's right – give her some air," Mr. C. said as he got to the stage and knelt down beside them. "Paula, kneel down at her feet and elevate her legs a bit. And someone go grab that small pillow off the prop table for her head." He gently shook Cassie's arm as the actress began to open her eyes and look around. He applied a little pressure on her arm to indicate she she shouldn't move. "Just rest a minute. Catch your breath."

Someone brought the pillow, and Teagan grabbed it and carefully placed it under Cassie's head. Cassie turned to look her and smiled weakly. "Hey, sis, how'd I do?"

Tears welled up in Teagan's eyes. "You were fantastic. Now rest a minute. Don't mess with Mr. C." Teagan looked up at all the faces around her, and noticed that Brian had gone to stand next to Beth Newton, who stood there frozen with fear on her face. Teagan knew exactly how she felt. She made eye contact with Beth and softly said, "She's gonna be fine – it's okay." Beth nodded as Brian's hug got a bit tighter.

"Does anyone have a juice box with them? Cassie needs some sugar in her system."

"I do!" yelled one of the sophomores. "I'll go and get it."

Mr. C. looked up and addressed the cast. "Everyone take five. Don't go far – we'll get started again in just a few." Cast members slowly moved back, some heading to the first row in the audience while other lingered around the stage watching the scene before them. He turned his attention back to Cassie.

"How ya doin', kid? Wanna try to sit up?"

Cassie nodded, and they slowly helped her to a sitting position. Teagan sat behind her, and guided Cassie's shoulders. "Here, lean on me for a minute until you get your bearing."

"I'm sorry, Mr. C." Cassie stammered. "That's never happened before."

"It's okay," he answered, patting her leg. "I'm just glad your friend here grabbed you before you hit your head."

Teagan felt her face flush a bit. Mr. C had just called her Cassie's *friend*. It was the first time she'd heard the term in reference to Cassie, and she realized that she really liked the acknowledgement. She had somehow come to see this snotty fat-phobic person as her friend. And as she recognized all the misjudgments she had made, she truly hoped that Cassie had come to see her in the same way.

One of the cast returned with a juice box, and Teagan gently handed it to Cassie. "Drink this," she directed. "You need some energy back in your system." She saw Cassie start to protest, and continued, "Cassie, it's okay. It's just juice – and your body's telling you it really needs something after all that dancing you did."

Cassie nodded as she took the box. "That's when I started feeling dizzy."

"I know," Teagan replied. "I was watching from the sides and I could see it a bit when you landed."

Mr. C. remained kneeling alongside them, running his hand through his hair as he decided how to continue. "Cassie," he began, "do you think you have the energy to make it down to the first row?" She nodded and began to move, but he stopped her. "No, no...finish your juice. But I'm thinking that we have two options. We can get you down to the first row, and then Ann can sit with you until your folks come—"

"No! I don't wanna leave – I'll be fine, Mr. C."

"*Or....*," he continued, "We could have you sit in the front row and watch the rest of rehearsal if you're feeling up for it. Different cast members can sit with you to make sure you're okay. But I don't want you doing any more scenes tonight. We can run through them without you up there. Happens all the time in theater. At least in rehearsals."

Cassie nodded, her lower lip trembling a bit. "But won't it be really hard for the others if I'm not on stage? I could just stand there and move slowly..."

Mr. C. shook his head. "You need to rest up for opening night, okay?"

Teagan had a thought. "Wait. I have an idea. If it really would be easier to have someone take over Cassie's role just for tonight, I know someone who could do it. I think she has all the songs and lines memorized, because she's run lines with me."

Mr. C. looked at her, waiting for a name.

"Beth Newton. I know she's only a freshman, Mr. C., but just for tonight, I don't think you'd be disappointed."

Cassie looked doubtful. "She's good, but I don't think that would work—"

Teagan interrupted. "If she sat with you in between scenes, you could guide her through it. Just for tonight. We need *you* for opening night." Cassie nodded quietly.

Mr. C. ran his hand over his mouth, considering the substitution. "I admit it would be easier to have someone playing the part. Let's ask her – but first, Teagan, can you and Paula help her down to the first row?" They both nodded, and in no time had Cassie settled in to her seat. Julia and Kyleigh came right over to sit with her and offer their support.

Teagan went and found Beth sitting with a couple of her friends, but Brian had stayed with her, knowing how hard the episode had been. When Beth saw Teagan approaching, she stood up and hugged her.

"I was so scared. It was like Joanne all over again."

"I know, sweetie, I was scared, too," Teagan held Beth's shoulders as she looked at her directly. "But she's okay, and we'll deal more that that later. Right now, Mr. C. wants to get back to rehearsal. And he wants you to take over Cassie's part, just for tonight."

"Me?" Beth asked incredulously. "But that part is—"

"You know every song and dance – and you have her lines almost memorized."

Brian had heard the conversation, and came up to break in.

"Absolutely! Beth, I know you can do it. What do you say?"

"I.....guess. But God, I'm nervous."

Teagan gave her a squeeze. "You'll be fine. And Cassie said she'd help you. Okay?"

Beth nodded, and Teagan could see some excitement growing in her eyes. She turned to find Mr. C. watching, and gave him a thumbs up sign. He nodded and stood up to address the cast.

"Okay, folks, break time is over." The cast immediately quieted down and gave him complete attention. "First of all, I want to thank you all for handling yourselves like professionals. Cassie had a fainting spell -- it happens sometimes under the bright lights – but she's okay." The cast clapped and a Teagan heard a few supportive comments being directed at Cassie.

Mr. C. continued. "Since we're off tomorrow night, I told Cassie I wanted her to just watch tonight so she can rest up for opening. That being said, we know she's a major lead, and that makes it harder for others on stage without her there. Cassie's going to sit in the front row and guide us along, but there's someone in the cast that can jump in and get through the basics of the character without too much trouble. Beth Newton," he said as gestured toward her, "has agreed to step in as a sub for tonight." Again the cast responded with light clapping and cheers.

"For those of you who are featured dancers – you'll need to do a few dances on your own if Beth's filling for Cassie in that scene, so keep that in mind. Aside from that, we're gonna start back up with the next scene, and continue on through the show. After rehearsal, stick around for some quick notes, but then I want everyone out of here early to rest up for opening. Got it? Okay, then lets get into places!"

Teagan and Beth stopped by Cassie on the way to the stage. Teagan was relieved to see Cassie smile at Beth and say, "Thanks for helping. I appreciate it."

Beth's eyes got wide with both excitement and nervousness. "Thanks....especially for letting me sit with you when I'm not on stage so you can give me tips." Cassie smiled and nodded, and Beth headed off to get into place. Cassie reached for Teagan's hand.

"Hey, thanks for catching me," she said.

Teagan gave her hand a squeeze. "Never thought I'd be saying this, but that's what friends do."

Cassie gave a little nod. "Break a leg, sis."

Teagan turned and headed back stage with a heart filled with love. She knew the rehearsal would go fine with Beth stepping into Cassie's role, and she was grateful that Cassie was okay after fainting. She had no doubt that there would be a conversation after the show about Cassie's health, but for the first time she felt that maybe Cassie would be receptive to help. And that was enough for the moment.

CHAPTER 22

Several nights later, the final show came to an end. Teagan received a standing ovation when she came out for her bow, and she could see Ida in her wheelchair in the front row, along with Cassie's family, Brian's mom, and her own parents. She wasn't sure exactly where they were sitting, but she knew that Charlotte Hurd, Karen Drake, and Maggie Richmond had brought Melvin, Kitty, and Gladys along as well. And sitting in the front row further down she could see Beth's parents, beaming with pride as they clapped for both their own daughter and Teagan.

As the cast took their final bows and the curtain closed, she was immediately surrounded by those she had come to love over the past couple of months. Mike, Cassie, Brian, Beth, and Paula all came up for a huge group hug, and tears flowed freely as personal hugs were exchanged. Teagan realized that she had been accepted by this wonderful cast of peers – no longer seen as the "fat girl", or the "weird girl" who didn't know what romance was. She was just Teagan….a confident, positive, sarcastic and down to earth friend. And her heart was full.

Beth found her among the crowd and gave her a huge hug. "Thank you SO much," she said. "Especially for the other night – having a chance to play your sister on stage was something I'll never forget." Teagan hugged her back hard, fighting back tears. "You'll always be my sister, kiddo," she whispered into her ear. "And your real sis must be so proud of you."

"Of both of us," Beth replied. She glanced around, making sure no one was listening. "And hey, Cassie and I talked the other night after rehearsal. I'll tell ya about it soon."

Brian came to hug her next. "God, you were sensational. I'm so glad we have one more year to do this again."

"Me, too," Teagan answered, realizing it was true.

As the crowd slowly diminished and headed toward the dressing rooms to change, Cassie lingered behind.

"Can you wait a sec?" she asked. Teagan could see that she looked worried, and her hand was cold to her touch.

"You okay?" Teagan asked, her face filling with concern. "Your hands are cold as ice." She led her over to to a small bench by the back of the stage and grabbed a blanket off a nearby chair. "Wrap yourself up in this to warm up a minute." She gently placed the blanket around her shoulders and sat down facing her.

Cassie held the blanket with one hand and reached out for Teagan's hand with the other. "I really need to talk to you, but I'm not sure when I might see you again after we leave tonight."

"Cassie," Teagan said gently,"You'll see me whenever you want. I really want to hang out and get to know you better. I mean that."

Cassie's eyes filled with tears. "When I first moved here I felt like everything was out of control, and I was totally alone."

"That had to have been hard, adjusting to a whole new world."

Cassie nodded. "When I found the studio, the dancing helped. But then I started comparing myself to everyone there, and I was doubting everything, you know?"

Teagan nodded, waiting for Cassie to continue.

Cassie swallowed hard, and her voice dropped to a whisper. "Beth told me about Joanne. And why she died." Her gaze met Teagan's and her eyes were full of tears. "And I don't want that to happen to me."

Teagan wrapped her arms around her as the tears came, holding

Cassie's thin body as she sobbed. "The other night......I've never fainted before.......and I'm really scared....." Cassie tried to speak through her sobs, but Teagan stroked her hair and tried to calm her.

"Ssh.....it's okay," she murmured. "It's gonna be okay."

When Cassie's body had calmed down, Teagan leaned back so she could look directly at her. "I've been wanting to talk to you about it for a long time, but we didn't exactly hit it off, did we?"

Cassie shook her head. "You scared me. It's like a couple of times when you looked at me I could tell that you knew. You really *did*, didn't you? Because of Joanne."

"I'd known her all my life, so I knew something was wrong with her. But as things got worse she got stubborn and pulled away. It still hurts that I couldn't save her."

Cassie wiped her tears. "Look, I know I need help. Well – sometimes. Other times I tell myself everything's fine and I'm in control. But after talking to you and Beth, I know it's a lie. I just don't know what to do."

Teagan squeezed her hands, noticing that some warmth was returning to them. "Listen, there's so much help out there for eating disorders today. And being open to that help – especially early on – is huge. But let's save that for another day, okay? Tonight let's just focus on the show and celebrate how good it was. And I know there's a certain lady sitting there out there who's really waiting to see both of us."

Cassie stood up, reaching for Teagan's hand. "You're right. Let's go out and see her. And I'm sorry I was so mean to you in the beginning. I like to think that maybe now we've...."

Teagan finished her thought for her. "Become friends?"

Cassie nodded and gave her a little hug. "Let's go find my gram."

CHAPTER 23

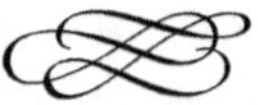

*D*uring the following week Teagan enjoyed getting back to her normal routine. She was grateful as peers approached her in the hallways or during class to complement her performance. She and Brian found that lunch time was at a bigger table now with some of their cast mates. While Brian sat next to Lou, Teagan was happy to have Cassie beside her. They had talked a few times since the show ended and were discovering just how much they had in common.

Even so, the topic of Cassie's anorexia had not come up since the closing night performance. Teagan knew it was was coming, but she didn't want to ruin their budding friendship. *"Just a little time to help us get to know each other better,"* she thought as she headed to work. *"Maybe Ida will have some news."*

As she headed back to work at Caldwell Manor Melvin met her at the door and started clapping. "Our star is back!"

"Thanks, Melvin. I'm so glad you were able to come and cheer me on."

They walked down to the activity room where most of the regulars were waiting for her. Kitty got up and started dancing and singing "Another opening, another show..." while Gladys clapped and tapped

166

her toes. Teagan laughed and looked around at all of them with such love.

"You guys are the best audience I've ever had. But how about we pull out the instruments and all sing some tunes together." As music filled the room other residents began to wander in as the sounds wafted down the hallway. Teagan was thrilled to see Ida wheeled into the room and join the circle right away instead of sitting off to one side. She really had become one of the resident leaders, and her positive attitude about aging and life had helped other residents as they transitioned from living at home to being at Caldwell Manor. Ida winked at her as the songs continued, and the next hour passed quickly with music and trivia and reminiscing of past days.

As the singalong ended many residents headed back to their rooms for a little quiet time before dinner. Teagan loved this last hour as she was able to spend time with individuals, and today she eagerly pulled a chair up beside Ida when things had quieted down.

"I'm so glad you came down today. I've missed you so much."

"Everyone here has missed you, I think. But those of us who saw you on stage have given five star reviews to residents and staff all week. You truly were just amazing, my dear."

"Thanks, Ida. It was one of the best things I've ever done. And I have to say, it really brought Cassie and I together at last. I think we're both looking forward to seeing where this friendship takes us."

Ida's eyes filled with tears. "My two favorite people in the world – friends at last. My heart is so full."

"Mine, too. But I'm a little scared, too. I don't know if Cassie told you about her fainting spell."

"She did, actually. She and Eliana came to visit together on Sunday morning, and we had a long talk about what had happened those last few days before the show."

"I'm so glad she told you. I was afraid I'd have to tell you and then she'd get all mad again."

"It was the first time Cassie's talked honestly about her problem, and she seemed open to getting the help she needs."

"I sure hope so, Ida. I really like her, and I think she's the friend that Joanne wanted me to have. But I'm not sure I'm strong enough to go through losing someone again. Sometimes I just wanna step back and wait to see if Cassie's really serious or just playing a game."

"What do you mean, my dear?"

"When Joanne's anorexia started getting really bad, she used her acting skills to keep it hidden. And she knew how to manipulate those of us that knew her best."

"Well Cassie seemed genuinely willing to get help. I think the fainting spell scared her. And she said she had talked to that younger sister of your friend, and that made a huge difference."

"That was Beth, and I'm so proud of her for opening up. I think seeing Cassie faint just made her determined to try and help. And if she was really able to get to her then that will help in her own healing, I'm sure."

Before Ida could reply Charlotte Hurd walked into the room. "Glad to find both of you here. I just got off the phone with Eliana, and we've scheduled a family meeting tomorrow afternoon. She asked that we could meet here so that both of you could be there."

"I assume this is about Cassie?"

Charlotte nodded. "The sooner we can intervene and talk about treatment the more likely we'll be able to get it started. Rather than start with a counselor Cassie didn't know, Eliana wanted to meet with those that know her best. They asked me to attend because of my medical background. Teagan, they'd really like you to attend if you can."

"I can't say that I know her all that well yet, but I'd be happy to come."

Ida reached out and patted her hand. "It will help, believe me. Cassie spoke a lot about you the other day when she came."

"I'm glad. I'll help however I can."

Charlotte checked her watch and turned to go. "We'll meet in the library at 3:00 so that we're not all crowded in my office. I asked Maggie Richmond to join us as well."

"Maggie? Does she even know Cassie?"

"She's met her a couple of times when Cassie's been in to visit. I think she might have some valuable input to the situation."

"I'm not sure Cassie will open up as much if someone she doesn't know is there," Teagan replied.

"Well, with Maggie's own battle with anorexia I thought she'd be a good person to have there. But right now it's just about time for dinner, and your shift is about over, so I think I'd better get Ida down the hall."

Ida smiled and backed her wheelchair up a bit. "I'll never be late for dinner! And I'll see you tomorrow, my dear. Let's pray that Cassie is truly ready for help."

"Trust, me, Ida. I've been praying that for weeks."

CHAPTER 24

Teagan arrived at Caldwell Manor as soon as school let out the next day. As her mom dropped her off they saw the "old curmudgeon" standing on the sidewalk next to his car. Maggie was chatting with him, and he shook his head in response to something just as a tow truck pulled up.

"Looks like Mr. Pritchard is having car trouble," Teagan said. "And it looks like Maggie got an earful with whatever he said."

Her mom chuckled. "Doesn't everybody he talks to? Give me a call when you're ready for a ride home. And good luck, honey."

"Thanks, mom. I might need it. I haven't felt this nervous since auditions."

She joined Maggie as they headed through the back door.

"Hope you didn't have to deal with Old Man Pritchard too long. Looks like he was his cheerful self."

Maggie laughed. "I'm used to it. I live right around the corner from him and see him every day while walking my dog. I think he's got a soft spot under that gruff exterior."

Charlotte was just inside. "Who has a soft spot?"

Maggie gestured out the door. "Mr. Pritchard. His car broke down outside and I was chatting with him a minute before the tow truck arrived."

"Aw, the Old Curmudgeon. You should have had him wait inside. It's still kind of chilly out there."

"I tried, Charlotte. He said he'd never walk through these doors again. Not sure what he meant, but he was adamant."

Charlotte glanced out the window at the old man climbing into the tow truck and smiled. "I know what he meant. I first met Carl when I had just started working here – over fifteen years now. His wife lived here the last few years she was alive. I don't think he ever missed a day without visiting. Even as her mind slipped away and she didn't know him anymore, he was here."

"Wow, he must have really loved her," Teagan replied.

"He adored her. He's hasn't really been the same since she died. I'm glad he didn't have to wait long for the tow truck. This place doesn't have a lot of happy memories for him. So, are you ready for the meeting?"

"As ready as we can be, I guess. Is Cassie here yet?"

"They should be arriving any minute. That's why I was waiting by the door. Why don't you two head into the library. I left Ida there just a minute ago. We'll join you as soon as they arrive."

Teagan and Maggie followed her suggestion and joined Ida in the library and Teagan was glad to sit next to her in the circle of chairs. Ida reached out and grasped her hands as she sat down. "I'm so grateful to have you here, my dear. I hope this meeting is the beginning of Cassie's recovery."

"Me, too, Ida. More than I can say."

Voices in the hallway signaled the arrival of Cassie and her parents, and Teagan smiled as she entered the room. Cassie gave a weak smile in return. "Hey, I didn't know you were gonna be here." She gave Teagan a quick hug and then another to Ida. "Hi, Gram. How are you today?"

"Glad to have you here, my dear. And how are you?"

"Kinda nervous to be here at all. I'm not really sure why we all had to meet."

Eliana took the question as her cue to facilitate the meeting.

"Cassie, after what happened last week, we thought it might be a good idea to meet all together to talk things over and give you our support. I think we're all relieved that you've finally admitted that you have a problem."

Cassie squirmed a bit in her chair next to Teagan. "Yeah, I admitted it. I know I have some issues with food to deal with. But I don't think a big meeting was needed. We could have just talked at home. Or in Gram's room, like we did the other day."

"I know honey, but your grandmother thought we'd have more room here. And I asked Charlotte to join us since she's a nurse and might be able to answer any questions you might have."

Teagan could tell that Cassie was uncomfortable. She seen this defensive reaction many times while trying to reason with Joanne, and she reached out to touch Cassie's arm. "Look, I know it's hard with so many other people here, but we all wanna help. I know how scared you were the night you fainted, and then again after closing night. And it's okay to be scared."

Cassie pulled back from her. "I'm not scared. I'm a little ticked off that you all wanna gang up on me. Okay, I admit I fainted. I don't always eat enough. But that night was mostly because of the lights and costumes and the long rehearsal."

"Cassie, it was way more than that, and you know—"

"Look, I'll be better about taking care of myself, okay? Without all the extra rehearsals I have it under control again. But thanks for caring – really."

There was an awkward silence in the room as Cassie's defiance got stronger. Ida was the one who broke the tension. "Cassie, do you remember telling me about your talk with Beth Newton after that rehearsal? Because you seemed a lot more open to getting some help after that night."

Cassie's look softened a bit. "Gram—and you, Teagan—I know I told you both about that conversation, and yes, it helped me to see that I do have a problem with my food. And I don't wanna end up like Joanne. But now that I'm aware of it and I've admitted it it will be okay. I just need to be more careful and lighten up on on the exercise, that's all."

Charlotte had been sitting quietly through the meeting, but decided it was time to speak up. "Cassie, as a nurse, I know a lot about the medical issues of anorexia. And it's not quite as easy a fix as what you've described. Recovering from an eating disorder takes a lot of time and some major medical support. Without it, you very well *could* end up like Joanne."

Teagan watched Cassie glare at the nurse as her hands got tense in her lap. *"This is gonna be Joanne all over again,"* she thought. *"Maybe this was a mistake being here at all."*

Charlotte softened her tone but continued on. "Look, there's place over in Brentwood that's designed specifically to help with eating disorders. Your parents thought it sounded nice, and I did check to see if they had an open bed—"

Cassie stood up quickly. "*What?* A bed? You're gonna *send* me somewhere? Mom, you told me we'd find a counselor. Not a friggin' hospital or psych ward!"

Eliana stood up and tried to hug her daughter, but Cassie put her hands up to stop her. "I wanna go home. You guys don't know anything about what I need! Not a single one of you!"

"I do." All eyes turned toward Maggie, who had not spoken a word until now.

"You? I've only met you a couple of times. I don't even know why you're at this meeting. Who the hell are you to know anything about me?"

Maggie stood up as Eliana sat back down, and she took one step toward Cassie and looked directly at her.

"I know *exactly* what you're going through. I stayed in that facility for several months when I was just a little older than you are now, and have continued to see my counselor there ever since I left. Because I'm an anorexic – just like you are. And I'll be a recovering anorexic for the rest of my life. And so will you, unless you die first."

Cassie remained standing, but her shoulders dropped and her lips quivered a bit. "You? You're an anorexic? 'Cause you don't look that—"

"Skinny?" Maggie interjected. "Thank God I'm not. But I was when I went there. And I didn't go willingly at first. I went kicking and screaming like you are now." Teagan gestured for Maggie to take her seat, and Cassie quietly sat down next to the social worker.

"Look, Cassie," Maggie continued, "I wasn't there the night you fainted, but I fainted several time myself, and I want you to think back on how scary it was. Because those raw emotions? That's *real*. That's what you true self is feeling. This charade today is nothing but lies."

"It is not."

"Your brain is *lying* to you. Anorexia is a disease that lies to us and tells us that we're fine and in control while our bodies are starving from lack of nutrients. This disease will kill you, Cassie. It almost killed me. And it did kill Joanne."

Teagan watched as the raw emotions returned and Cassie's eyes watered up. She approached and knelt down next to her friend and grabbed her hand. "Maggie's right. I can tell that right now you're back to where you were after the show. And this is the Cassie that can get better – the real one."

"It just hurts. I don't wanna feel this scared anymore. And I don't wanna die."

Maggie put her arm around Cassie's shoulders. "You don't have to die. But you *do* have to get help. You can't fix this by yourself. You need people to help you learn how to face the fears and recognize the lies. I can tell you that the place in Brentwood will do that. But you need to be willing to fight. And that starts here – with surrendering amidst that fear."

"Can you do that, Cassie?" Teagan asked gently. "Can you do it for your folks, and your Gram, and for me? Because I don't want to lose another friend."

Cassie looked around the room at all the concerned faces, and nodded quietly through her tears. "Okay. I'll go." Her lips trembled as the sobs came again.

Maggie patted her back. "It's not an easy fight, but with help you can learn to live without being controlled by the anorexia. And I'll come to visit you any time you need to talk to someone who gets it."

"And you don't have to live with the fear anymore," Ida added, "Because you'll have lots of us with you every step of the way."

Cassie looked at her grandmother and smiled. "Thanks, Gram." She took a deep breath and squeezed Teagan's hand. "Will you be there, too?"

Teagan nodded and gave her friend a smile as she whispered back. "Of course I will. I promise."

ACKNOWLEDGMENTS

Special thanks to the following people:

To those who helped with big and small jobs in beta and sensitivity reading, editing, formatting, and overall support: Rebecca, Elle, Caitlin, and Melissa.

To my amazing cover designer Noel Sellon for bringing my imagined vision for Caldwell to life.

To Melissa Koberlein for her continued wisdom and support throughout the writing and publishing process.

To my fellow authors and writers of the Greater Lehigh Valley Writers' Group (GLVWG) for your input at writers' cafes and camaraderie at meetings and conferences. No one understands the crazy world of writing more than fellow writers!

To my at home writing buddy Rebecca — I think we barter well across the table from each other!

To the family and friends who support me with love and genuine caring throughout the process: Cheryl, Maria, Patti, Randi, Jackie, and Kerry. I love you all so much!

To my loving family — Bob, Beth, and Rebecca — who continue to be my reason for living.

ABOUT THE AUTHOR

Laurel Wenson grew up in the small town of Concord, Massachusetts. Her love of reading and books began in this town rich with the literary history of Thoreau, Emerson, Alcott, and Hawthorne. Caldwell is loosely modeled after this hometown and contains some of the author's favorite places: the library, the cemeteries, and a great little pizza shop.

A Promise to Keep is her debut novel, and those that know the author will recognize bits and pieces of her life story interwoven throughout. Laurel's career has included jobs of teacher, administrator, theater director, music therapist, and activity aide. She has been a fan of theater all her life, and has performed in many school and community productions, either as actress, director, music director, or accompanist.

Laurel's first book, *Sets on a Shoestring: How to Build Sets and Props on a Limited Budget,* was published in July of 2019. She has already begun drafting notes for her next Caldwell story.

She lives in the Lehigh Valley of Pennsylvania with her husband, two daughters, and two cats. She's a member of the Greater Lehigh Valley Writers Group and has served on the planning committee for the Write Stuff writers' conference that meets annually in Bethlehem, PA. For more information about the author visit her website or follow her on social media.

Website: laurelwenson.com

www.ingramcontent.com/pod-product-compliance
Lightning Source LLC
Chambersburg PA
CBHW071518100726
47908CB00004B/1209